The Looking Glass Labyrinth

by Judi Getch Brodman

The Looking Glass Labyrinth is dedicated to my dear parents, Kay and Charlie Getch, who always encouraged me to be and do my best. I've tried to live as my Dad urged me to – "have no regrets, no I should've, could've, or wished I had."

They are responsible for bringing me to Wellfleet as a very small child. This wonderful village, located on the northern tip of Cape Cod, is a spot that fills my mind and heart with memories of an antique white shingled house with green shutters, a cement patio that surrounded it on two sides, and a long winding driveway that hid the house and barn from Cove Road; days beginning with the raising of the American flag over the barn, and then a game of horseshoes played in the sunny sandy yard; low tide afternoons digging shellfish from Chipmans Cove's muddy bottom; and, family cookouts on the beach in the glow of glorious sunsets followed by concerts in the cottage orchestrated by the mesmerizing and magical player piano. Bedtime brought the long steep climb up the stairs to a single, large, often hot and sultry dormitory style bedroom. The summers seemed endless then….

As my Father used to say, "Once you have the sand and salt water in your blood, you are forever part of Wellfleet," and he was correct. When I'm in Wellfleet, I love it, when I'm not there, I write about it.

How could I not make this precious little historic village the setting of my novels? Enjoy Wellfleet and Rose Hill as you turn the pages of *The Looking Glass Labyrinth*.

Chapter One

Flipping to the yard sale section of the newspaper, Rachael Corbet pulled out a red pen from her purse and circled ads while her friend, Kayla Simon, signaled the waitress for her third coffee refill.

"And as I said for the umpteenth time, he asked for you." Kayla stopped. "Hello? I said Stan Talbot's interested in you."

"So?" Rachael ignored her, tapping her red pen on the table and scanning the page.

"So? That's your answer when our hunky town doctor asks for you? Hell, he'd already be on my speed dial."

"I have no doubt," Rachael countered as she stirred her coffee. "I've circled about ten promising yard sales for today."

"Listen to me." Kayla's voice rose with each word, causing people in the Village Coffee Shoppe to turn. "It's been five years. He's not coming back."

"Shhh," Rachael leaned in and whispered. "Stop it, Kay. Please, don't give me your 'move on' lecture again." Kayla's blunt words hurt. Rachael had tried with little success to shut away that time in her life.

"So, now you're going to be a nun?" Kayla declared in her grandmother's Yiddish accent, making Rachael smile. Kayla was Jewish; Rachael a Catholic, but neither of them had seen the inside of a temple or church in a long while. That wasn't the only difference between them— Kayla was dark haired with an olive complexion and rich brown eyes, slightly plump and short. Rachael on the other hand stood 5'9" in her stocking feet, had long naturally curly red hair that framed fair skin and sea green eyes perfectly, and a reed thin body from running.

"Hey, there could be worse life choices," Rachael answered quickly, "I've thought of it." She bit her lip to keep from being sucked into yet another discussion about Vince, especially here in public. Kayla didn't understand, and Rachael couldn't explain. She circled another yard sale, drawing an asterisk next to it. "Look, here's an interesting one, a yard sale at Rose Hill."

"You're kidding, right? That ugly shrek of a house on the hill? Ghost Haven?"

"Starts at 10AM. Says they're selling off their seafaring ancestors' belongings." Rachael took another sip of her coffee. "You have your computer? Can you Google it and see if there's anything interesting about it?" Rachael, a writer, avoided her computer as much as possible on her days off. Kayla, for some reason, was never without hers.

Kayla pulled up a website describing the historical eighteenth century home. "First, the photo must have been taken a hundred years ago—it sure doesn't look like that now." She kept on reading. "It says here that the house of horrors was built in the 1700's by a seafaring merchant and has been boarded up for years and if I had to guess, by the looks of it, probably since the 1700's. What in the world do you want from there? Although," she added, "who knows, maybe they're selling the gun that killed the infamous sea captain."

"I doubt they referred to it as 'the house of horrors.' You're so cruel. No wonder you can't find a date – whose skin's that thick." Rachael knew that she had pricked Kayla's soft spot.

Tweaking each other came naturally since the first day that they had met as kids in middle school outside of Boston. It was gym class and Kayla flew off the horse like a pro right onto the mat where Rachael was attempting her floor exercise routine; they collided, rolled and laughed themselves silly, blaming each other for not watching out where they were going. That theme had kept them close friends through the years—watching out for where the other one was heading.

"What time do you have?" Rachael asked.

"Nine-thirty, why?"

"Just checking. I don't want to be late for this once in a lifetime estate sale. Want to come?" Rachael raised one eyebrow as she often did when she was joking. "We may never have another chance to see the inside of that house again," she taunted.

"You're really serious? You're actually going inside? You know what they say, right? That she still takes nightly strolls through the halls looking for her captain? The lights that people see in the windows?"

"Really? Are the 'they's' on your computer or in your head?" Rachael laughed, pleased with her jab. "I never realized you believe in ghosts. And I'm not going there at night, I'm going now."

"I don't exactly believe in supernatural stuff, but it's 180 degrees from the logical engineering crap I deal with every day. By the way, when I drove by Ghost Haven last week, I saw a woman digging in the side jungle. When I looked again, she was gone. It's haunted, Rachael, I'm serious, it's really haunted. Ask anyone in town."

"No one knows what really happened to that sea captain, only that he was shot and killed inside the house hundreds of years ago. Sounds like I could pick up some unique background material for my writing." Rachael could never pass up a good mystery. "And maybe he roams through the house during the day. I bet he's very handsome," Rachael teased. "Now, he might be a good catch for me."

"You're crazy, you really are. The article says that there are two 'grandchildren-cubed'."

"You coming or not?"

"Not on your life." Kayla slid her iPad into her backpack while Rachael paid the bill. Outside the restaurant, Kayla said, "I know you. This is a ploy so you don't have to talk about Stan or Vince."

Rachael didn't bite. "Talk later. And if you're really lucky, maybe I'll invite you over later for a beer and you can drool all over my great treasures including the Rose Hill captain." She waved her hands in the air making a ghostly noise.

"Rose Hill, my ass. Ghost Haven."

"Talk later. Say hi to Stan for me," Rachael called out from her aqua colored Mini Cooper convertible. "Do you want me to pick out something for you?" she called back as she pulled away. She never heard Kayla's answer, but could only imagine what it was.

Chapter Two

Damn Kayla, why did she always have to be correct? There wasn't another soul parked in front of the decaying, shuttered, ancient...haunted house. Even the rusty old black wrought-iron gate had rusted off its hinges and stood leaning against the contorted remains of the fence, making it look like a musical staff. Maybe this time she should have listened to Kayla's warning.

As hard as it was to believe, Kayla was often the voice of reason. Take Bermuda for example—they were college juniors on spring break and Rachael had wanted to prove that she was fearless, needed to show Vince a photo of her on a motor bike. Kayla refused to go near the 'death machine', as she quaintly called it. So Rachael rode off alone and an hour later called Kayla from the hospital after skidding on a corner and skinning her knee on suspected coral. With antibiotics in hand and a bandage on her knee, Rachael had finished spring break quietly on the beach. But Vince had loved the photo.

"Okay Kay, you win, I've wasted enough time here," Rachael said in disgust. She scanned the other circled estate notices in the newspaper. There was a late 1800's era sea captain's house a street over that looked promising. With a little luck, she might find something to jump start her writing juices again. Usually snooping through old houses and people's possessions or 'junk' as Kayla called it produced a seed for a story. Maybe she could write a Halloween story using Ghost Haven as the backdrop.

She threw the newspaper down on the front seat and started to back up when she saw it—the unobstructed views of Cape Cod Bay, Wellfleet Harbor and Duck Creeke, all woven together like a beautiful sky blue, azure, and marsh green patchwork quilt.

She shut off the car, leaned back and watched the white boats anchored at the pier stretch out like tiny irregularly sized pearls on a string; seagulls circle over an incoming fishing boat; a sailboat floats by on a whisper of wind. Even two hundred years ago, someone had chosen the perfect spot for their home.

"Crap," she whispered, smacking the steering wheel. "Excuse my French, but really, is this what you're throwing at me?" she turned back to the old neglected house. "Okay, just for the sake of argument, let's say that I've always loved you. If I overlook your ghosts, decaying clapboards, shuttered windows, and falling down fences, what else do you have to offer?" She scanned the Harbor.

"Alright, I agree the view's awesome, but have you looked at yourself lately?" Rachael questioned the antique lady. "Truly, you must see it. I know, you say you were gorgeous in your day, but we both know that ship sailed a long time ago. I hate to be the one to break it to you, but you haven't aged well. I know, I know, not your fault, but still, neglect has taken its toll." Dilapidated shutters hung off the windows, exposing the once cream colored paint that peeled from the rotting clapboards. "You know the position you're putting me in, don't you? I'll never hear the end of this from Kay."

Rachael studied the aristocratic structure again. Her college architecture classes had provided her with a love of eighteenth century buildings from their soft honey colored wide pine floors to kitchens with huge brick fireplaces and tall sun grabbing windows. Sea captains' homes were even more special with widow's walks where the wives could stand and watch for incoming ships. Rose Hill's walk had rotted away with its railings lying in the weeds next to the crumbling veranda. Yes, she had been a beauty in her day, for sure.

"I'm crazy, I know, but you've persuaded me to go in. You better make it worth my while, that's all I have to say. You hear me?"

Rachael checked her watch—ten minutes to wait. She let the warmth of the spring sunshine wash over her winter body as her mind wandered back to her earlier conversation with Kayla. She thought that Vince's death haunted Rachael because she had loved him so much. The truth be told, she wasn't sure that she had loved him enough. And not a soul knew that, not even her best friend. The guilt wrapped itself so tightly around her heart sometimes that she felt like she could hardly breathe.

Dear, sweet Vince. She smiled as she remembered how she had stumbled upon him, literally. She was a junior in high school. Kayla had christened her a klutz and Rachael had proven her correct that day. She tripped. In doing so, she had unleashed the contents of her backpack from one side of the school corridor to the other. There she sat on her fanny, skirt up, and tights ripped.

Vince, the senior quarterback, had unfortunately been in the line of fire. He stopped short just as her books flew by him.

"Wow… incoming," he joked. "You're kidding me, this stuff's all yours? How'd you carry it?" He offered his hand as she struggled to stand.

Rachael babbled something about loving to read, all the while evading his look as she smoothed her skirt and restored her flaming red hair back into a ponytail. She was shy, serious, and an A student; Vince was outgoing, funny, and a handsome football star. He towered over her, had a killer smile, and made her blush when he read her name from the cover of her notebook.

"Rachael Corbet, why haven't I seen you at the football games? I'd remember that red hair for sure."

She knew who he was, every girl in school talked about him. "I… I… I don't really understand football," she stammered. As soon as the words fell out of her mouth, she heard her mother's admonition, "Sometimes girl, you are just too truthful."

His laughter caused every kid at their locker to turn, embarrassing Rachael even more.

His stare made her uneasy. "I don't have time for silly things like that," she answered angrily, slipping her glasses into her pocket. He was making fun of her. She slammed her books into her backpack one by one. She had never been so mortified in her entire life. Everyone in the corridor was watching and probably heard his ridiculing laugh. All she wanted to do was run out of school and never come back.

"Hold on," he said, reaching out for her book bag. "I didn't mean to make you mad. In fact, I have a proposition, Rachael Corbet," he offered, picking up the rest of her books. He tucked a loose tendril of hair behind her ear.

She looked away, feeling the heat return to her face.

"Let's see if this'll work," he added, walking her toward the door. "Since I don't have time for my English assignments and you love that stuff so much, would you tutor me? But," he added, placing his finger against her lips to keep her from speaking, "there's a catch. In return, I get to teach you about football and you come to my games. Deal?"

She felt dizzy, tongue tied. Her heart pounded. She nodded. "Deal."

And so, they studied together in the school library a few late afternoons a week after Vince's football practice. She enchanted him with her ability to bring the writings of the great authors to life. And he captured her mind with his skillful drawings of football plays with X's and O's. On game day, he reserved a seat right behind his bench, so when he ran off the field, he could easily spot her. Her thumbs up made him smile. Oh, how she had loved his smile.

Vince passed his English course with flying colors, his team racked up an undefeated season with him at the helm, and Rachael became an avid football fan. His sweet gentle kiss as they studied Elizabeth Browning's love poems had captured her heart and mind—it was her first.

He took her to his senior prom and then, in September, left for Michigan on a well-deserved football scholarship. They agreed that they could see others. She dated a few guys in her class, but they somehow seemed too immature for her. Vince told her that he wasn't interested in dating anyone but her. She loved him, but was too young to believe that her first love could be her true love.

At the end of his senior season, the Pittsburgh Steelers drafted him. When Vince graduated, he enlisted in the army as three generations of his family before him had. "The Steelers can wait," he told her, "the war can't."

At the airport terminal as they waited for his unit to be called to board their flight to Afghanistan, he dropped to one knee, flipped open a black velvet box, and asked her to marry him. Everyone cheered; Rachael cried; Vince picked her up and twirled her around whispering that he would love her forever. He said that he needed to know that she would wait for him. He quoted "Lizzy Browning" as he had called her in high school. "How do I love thee…"

Rachael threw back her head, laughing through her tears. Some of her tutoring had actually stuck. She hugged and kissed him and accepted his ring, but somewhere deep inside, she had questioned whether she would keep it or give the ring back when he returned. She never had to decide.

About six months into his tour, Vince's sister, Vanessa, phoned with news that he had been severely injured. Rachael left her classes at Simmons College and flew to Germany to be with him. After a month, he died, never having regained consciousness, save for those last few moments before the end. She returned to school, threw herself into finishing her classes and had done some of her best writing. But somehow everything felt so different— she had grown up.

In a way, she had been relieved that she hadn't said anything to him about her doubts. Then, as the days and weeks dragged by, she wondered if she had stolen precious time from him, time that he could have used to find someone else. She smiled, knowing that he never would have looked for someone else because he had called her the love of his life.

Five years had passed and she still hadn't found anyone to fill the empty hole that he had left inside her. Actually, she hadn't really tried. Vince was a tough act to follow.

A clattering noise shook her out of the past. She wiped away the tears that dripped down her cheeks with the cuff of her sweater. Someone on the top floor had thrown open the rickety shutters—most likely Kayla's ghost seeking some fresh air. She checked her watch and saw it was almost ten.

Damn Kayla, she thought as she made her way up the overgrown path. She might be correct again. Maybe it was time for her to move on.

Chapter Three

"Hello? Anyone here?" Rachael poked her head inside the dark gloomy hallway as she knocked. The hoarse gong of a grandfather clock hidden in the shadows croaked ten o'clock.

"Hello," she called again as she pushed the creaky wooden carved doors open. A long dark dank corridor stretched out before her. A shaft of light crossed the dirty pine floors from what must have been the formal living room.

She sighed. She had hoped the house inside might be in better condition—it wasn't. The deteriorated outside was bad enough, but the dark, depressing, bleak inside had been neglected for centuries as well. Taking out her phone, Rachael snapped a photo of the misty mid-morning sun as it filtered through the tattered sheer draperies and the dirty windows. With a few clicks, she sent it off to Kayla with the words, "See what you're missing!"

Rachael tugged her sweater tightly around her body as a cold draft blew over her. *Kay said that's what you feel when a ghost enters a room. Didn't she also say that the ghost only roamed at night?* The shabby curtains swayed.

Rachael turned and faced a portrait of a young woman, her curly blond hair pinned on top of her head, hanging above the boarded up fireplace. The filtered sunlight illuminated her face making her appear alive. As Rachael moved toward the painting, the crystal blue eyes eerily followed her.

"Was it you blowing that cold wind? Trying to scare me? Or maybe you didn't like me snapping the picture? Smile." Rachael hesitated for a second before pressing the button. The woman appeared so real in her lens, donning an all-knowing smile. *Click.*

"My great-great-great-grandmother," a female voice behind her offered.

"Oh my God." Rachael's phone slipped out of her hand and crashed to the floor. "I didn't realize anyone else was here. I'm sorry. The door was open, it was ten o'clock so when no one answered, I just let myself in," she babbled, retrieving her phone from the dusty wide plank floor and wiping it on her sweater.

The tiny woman dressed in dirty jeans, an oversized plaid jacket, and no shoes had managed to enter the room without making a sound—like a ghost. Her scads of blonde curly hair refused to be controlled in the bun on the top of her head, creating a halo around her flushed cheeks. This must be the woman Kayla had seen working in the garden. How disappointed she would be to know her ghost was a live person.

"I'm sorry. I can delete the photo if you like. I'm actually here for the estate sale." She reached into her back jean's pocket and retrieved the folded newspaper ad.

Estate sale - Come wander through Rose Hill, a Victorian home built in 1754 by the Johnston family, filled with artifacts from their sailing days. Doors open Saturday at 10AM.

The woman waved Rachael's apology off, faced her ancestor and joked, "I'm sure she enjoyed a little human interaction after being locked up here alone for so many years. By the way, I'm Sarah. I saw you sitting in your car when I unlocked the upstairs shutters." She wiped her hands on her jeans. "Please, take your time and look around. All the pieces marked with red dots are for sale; all the unmarked, covered or boxed items stay."

"I understand." Rachael wondered why Sarah had used the present tense when speaking of the painted lady.

"And I'm Rachael. Nice to meet you, Sarah." She offered her hand.

Sarah ignored Rachael's extended hand, mumbled something about having dirt all over her, and rubbed her hands once again on her pants.

"Doesn't appear to be much of a rush to buy these old relics," Sarah declared, inferring that everything in the house was junk.

"Well, I'm here," Rachael stated, "hoping to discover something that I can't live without. I'm usually pretty lucky that way."

"Good luck. If you find anything like that here, you're certainly welcome to it," Sarah uttered and turned to walk away.

"Before you leave Sarah, can I ask you about the painting?" Rachael didn't wait for her to answer, "The woman is so lifelike. Is she the one that everyone talks about?"

"If you mean the ghost, yes. And interestingly enough, her name is also Rachael." She stood on her toes and reached up touching the painting's frame as though straightening it. Then, she turned and fastened her great-great-great grandmother's crystal blue eyes on Rachael. "What a coincidence, you both have the same name. I'm sure she brought you here to discover something that will touch your heart."

Her words chilled Rachael. It was like Sarah had read her mind. Maybe Kayla's instincts weren't so far off about this place.

"I wasn't trying to be disrespectful; it's just that this morning at breakfast, my friend read me a story about how she searches the hallways looking for her Captain. She mentioned that there had been sightings?" Rachael struggled to smooth over what she had said earlier.

"Sightings—absolutely. I know she's still here," she smiled up at the portrait.

"Really, you believe that?"

"For sure. I've found things moved around in the house. She exists, I have no doubt."

"Could you tell me a little more about her?" Rachael felt a connection to this woman in the painting for some reason, maybe because they shared the same name.

"Well, her story is simple. Rachael was born and died in this house. She fell in love with an older man whose first and only love was the sea. He died before they married, leaving her pregnant with his child. We think he was shot and killed in the hallway by the kitchen." She pointed to the corridor outside the parlor door.

"What happened, do you know?"

"You mean who killed him? I don't think anyone knows for sure. Some say that robbers broke into the house and he tried to fight them off. Some say that men who were jealous of him marrying Rachael came after him. Others say that she shot him in a rage because he wouldn't marry her, and there are even those who say his own men turned against him. Take your pick. All we know is that he left her pregnant and alone. She became the scarlet woman of her time."

"How terrible." Rachael studied the painting—the doll-like face, flushed with excitement, love and joy. "And she never married?"

"Never. She had his son, remained single, and became a recluse here at Rose Hill, running her father's shipping business." Sarah's words were clipped and angry.

"I'm sorry. She must have been very strong to take over her father's business and raise a son by herself at that time."

Sarah nodded. "I guess."

Rachael wanted Sarah to share more information about the woman, but after a few awkward seconds of silence, Rachael asked, "Are you selling the house as well?"

"We are. Well, let me rephrase that, I want to. Rachael's father built this house back in the eighteenth century and it has been passed down to my brother and me." Sarah scanned the room as if seeing it for the first time—the tattered couch, the dusty bookshelves and the well-used blackened fireplace.

"My brother talks about keeping it, but I want to sell—just look at this place, it's a disaster. Who could live here? Certainly not me." She shook her head as though in disgust. "I can't imagine why he wants to hold on to this mausoleum, he never spends any time here. Are you interested in buying it? I don't have a price, but maybe if he knows someone is interested, he would reconsider."

"I hadn't really thought about buying a permanent home, but Rose Hill is tempting." Sarah was moving way too fast for Rachael. "Can we discuss it after I've gone through the entire house?" Sarah seemed so removed from her roots. Why wouldn't she want to figure out who killed her ancestor? She sure would.

"Take your time. Just let me know when you're leaving so I can close up the house if no one else shows." Sarah started out the door and then turned back, saying, "Up the staircase at the end of the hallway are the bedrooms. Rachael's bedroom—well, I guess I'll have to call her 'Lady' since she was the lady of the house —is just as she left it. It's been locked up for years. We actually had to remove the door hinges to open it. No one could find the original key." She removed her gardening gloves from her back pocket and started to put them on. "Anyway, be careful walking through the rooms and along the hallways. The floors are warped and there's debris everywhere." She adjusted her dirt covered gloves, "I'll be digging up some of Lady Rachael's heirloom flowers. Call me if you need anything."

"Thanks," Rachael replied as Sarah disappeared.

She texted Kayla again, "You should be here—you'd love it!" If the dead were spooky, the living weren't far behind.

Chapter Four

The musty dark hallway held Lady Rachael's sea captain's secret somewhere under the layers and layers of peeling paint and wallpaper, but where? Only Kayla's ghost would know. Speaking of Kay, Rachael had to ask her why she hadn't bothered to tell her that the lady of the night was also named Rachael.

Kayla's voicemail picked up. "Simon says leave important information only, please." Rachael smiled. How wickedly perfect—a chance to spook Kayla. Rachael lowered her voice and whispered, "Kayla Simon, this is the resident spirit of Rose Hill—the one who carries the light at night? You've seen me, I know," Rachael hesitated dramatically, "because I've seen you." She hesitated again dramatically. "Your friend Rachael is here with me today. Interesting that we have the same name, don't you think? I have a task for her. At this moment, she's the only one who can change a bit of history for me. Don't worry, I'll return her in a few days unharmed —mostly." Rachael projected a deep laugh and shut off her phone.

"There you go, Kayla. Sounds like I've been hired to do some investigative work for Lady Rachael," she said, adopting Sarah's name for her, and pocketing the phone. She knew Kayla would attempt to call her back in a dither. She'd let her stew.

"Well, Lady Rachael, if you've picked me to solve your mystery, I'm in."

Rachael slid her hand along the wall looking for a bump or bulge. Something flashed ahead of her. When her eyes readjusted, there was nothing there but blackness.

"Hello? Anyone there?" Now she was seeing things, thanks to Kayla. She entered the room where the light had come from and walked to the French doors thinking that the flash may have come from outside. She pulled on the door handle; it was stuck. She stood stone still, her breathing the only sound filling the room.

"Damn you, Kayla." She was definitely in her head.

Rachael wiped a tiny spot on the dirty glass pane with the cuff of her sweater. Beyond the wide dilapidated wooden veranda was Sarah bent over in the weeds digging up what looked like irises roots, flowering quince bushes and a small forsythia plant and placing them in her wheelbarrow. Strange that she chose to concentrate all her energy into saving the plants with the house in such a deployable condition. The garden would certainly not sell this house.

Rachael circled the dark mahogany trestle table that monopolized the center of the dining room. Dragging her finger in the dust, she saw that the wood underneath still shone.

What looked like a large eighteenth century yellowed hand carved French chandelier hung above the table. Knowing from experience that real crystals resent human touch, she used the cuff of her sweater to rub one of the exquisitely hand carved tear drops. It lit up like a rainbow.

As she watched the colors dance off the walls, the French doors clanged open and a cold spring breeze blew through the room.

Rachael rewrapped her sweater and moved hurriedly to close the doors. "What the...? You were stuck a minute ago." Rachael slammed the doors shut and twisted the protruding rusty knob. It worked this time.

"So that's your answer, Lady Rachael?" Rachael stood defiantly with hands on her hips, waiting for a reply. "Don't think you can scare me off by blowing things around. Like it or not, I'm off to see the rest of the house," she threw over her shoulder heading out of the room.

She sidestepped the discarded cabinet doors and ripped up flooring as she picked her way through the back kitchen and up the steep dark stairs. Every step was an adventure.

"Well Sarah, you're right about one thing, a crew working here for months might make this place livable again." Rachael repeated what her father used to say. "But it does have good bones."

Fingering her way along the dark passageway on the second floor, she emerged into a room that resembled an indoor garden. The removed door leaned against the faded yellow rose wallpaper. A peach and yellow frayed upholstered chair stood near French doors that must have led to a balcony. A piece of wood lay across them.

"Your refuge, my Lady, for sure," Rachael whispered.

Facing west, covered with a tattered rose-colored quilt, was an ornate carved canopy bed that had a small worn wooden stepstool that protruded from the end just enough to make Rachael trip over it.

She laughed, catching her balance. "Still very much the klutz."

Nestled into the corner and sitting in front of a set of long paned windows stood a dusty honey colored wooden roll top desk. The chair, askew as if Lady Rachael had just arisen, afforded a perfect view of the entrance to Wellfleet harbor.

"If nothing else sells Rose Hill, this room will. I would die for this view," Rachael whispered. "You watched for your captain's ship to enter the harbor from here, didn't you?" she asked.

Looking down, she noticed a handwritten journal lying open on the desktop.

15 October 1878

I have only a little life left in this old body of mine. I'm tired tonight, very tired. Soon the winter cold will creep into the house. Now that Mazie has died, only old Carolyn and I are here in the house. I have survived too many seasons without my love—it is time for me to go home. I know that when I draw my last breath and take his hand, I will be smiling. I miss him so.

I have revisited the moment when I lost him over and over again, thinking of what might have been if he had not died that night, if I had been more vigilant, if I had stayed to help him. I guess, that was my punishment...

Rachael turned to the next page. It was blank. She must have died that night. Lady Rachael's final words read as though someone else had shot her lover. But her regrets rang loud and clear in Rachael's ears.

"There's no going back, no changing history, and no second chances, Lady Rachael. Women like us have to live with our guilt."

Rachael remembered how, every day on her way to the hospital, she would stop at the same coffee shop. As she stood at the counter, the owner would ask, "How's your soldier boy today?" in his heavy German accent as he made her coffee and wrapped her muffin.

"About the same," Rachael would answer. When she held out a five dollar bill, he would wave his hand and say, "He has paid enough for all of us." She thanked him and headed out the door, her eyes filled with tears. He was such a dear man.

One afternoon as she sat by Vince's side, his sister, Vanessa, arrived. She chatted about holding their wedding in the hospital room. Could that happen with him in a coma? Rachael asked the doctor. His look said it all. After a minute, he advised them to hold off on the wedding until he had a better prognosis.

"Right now it looks like if Vince recovers, and that's a big if, his injuries are so severe that he will require twenty-four hour care."

After Vanessa left, Rachael sat on Vince's bed, took his hand in hers and kissed his calloused finger tips. "You've been playing your guitar I see—a lot. I know I've told you this many times before, but I miss you so much. You kept me off balance from the first day we met." She laughed in spite of her tears, "Well, I guess I was off balance already that day. What did you ever see in me? I was a nerd and a klutz." She rubbed his hand along her cheek, watching him breathe with the aid of the respirator. He had no response. His ashen face showed no emotion. She pushed his hair back saying, "I always loved it when your hair was a tad too long. It made you look even sexier." She leaned down and kissed his cold pale cheek. "As if you could be any sexier."

Her words simply tumbled out. "I don't know what to do anymore, Vince. I know you and this is not how you would want to live...it's not the way I want you to live. You deserve better." She knew that if he had had the choice, he would have preferred death on the battlefield to living like this.

Her tears dribbled out. "You always talked about teaching your son, our son, how to play football." She blew her nose in a tissue that she grabbed from the box on his bedside table. "Look what you did with me...I'm a wizard now understanding all the plays. Okay, maybe not a wizard," she tried to joke. How she ached to hear one of his snappy replies. She wiped her tears with his bruised cold hand, laid her head on his chest, and wept. She heard the beat of his heart. "Please Vince...please help me."

All of a sudden, he squeezed her hand as though he knew what she was thinking and agreed with her.

She sat up. "What, what are you telling me? I love you, Vince."

He clasped her hand harder and then his hand went slack.

"No Vince, please…no, no please…. Nurse!" she yelled, as the monitor alarms sounded and the room filled with doctors and nurses. They shoved her out of the way as they proceeded to work on him—to no avail. The doctor approached her.

"No…no, he can't be gone." She tried to push past him as he held her shoulders. Rachael looked at him and sobbed that Vince had grasped her hand, twice. The doctor dismissed it as muscle spasms, but Rachael knew better. Vince had said goodbye.

"Lady Rachael, your guilt stemmed from not keeping your love alive while mine comes from wishing him dead." Rachael swiped at her tears.

"But I realize now that it's time for me to move on with my life and maybe you need to as well," she said remembering the promise that she had made when she entered the house. "Maybe if I solve the mystery of who killed your love, it will help us both to take the next step. I can live my life and you can rest easy in your death." She searched her pockets for a tissue but must have left them in the car. Seeing one of the desk drawers slightly ajar, Rachael yanked on it thinking maybe it held tissues. It wouldn't budge. Using both hands, she tugged harder on the handle until finally it gave way with a slow rasping noise.

There on top of a pile of old papers rested a framed sketch. Removing it, she placed it on the desk. Dark eyes with a mischievous glint gazed out at her. A knowing smile was slightly hidden by a dark trimmed beard.

She wiped her tears with her sweater sleeve. "So this is your gorgeous Captain. No wonder you fell madly in love with him, Lady Rachael. Well, I'll definitely need to borrow your diary if I'm to figure out who shot this handsome rogue." The French doors to the balcony clanked open, knocking over the piece of wood that had stood in front of them. The incoming wind flipped the pages of the diary.

"Oh, God, not again," she said, annoyed with yet another banging door. "Well, whoever buys this place will have to replace or fix all the doors." If Kayla had been here when they flew wide open, people in the village would have heard her screaming, "Get the hell out of here! Run...."

Rachael slammed the doors shut and, without thinking, plopped herself down in front of the diary. She wiped her hands on her jeans before touching the page that lay open before her. She read the words aloud:

I should have known better—should have acted differently. Why didn't I?

The rest of the page was blank. Rachael flipped back one page to the night that she thought that Lady Rachael had died. A minute ago, there was nothing further written in the diary. Rachael started to stand, but then sat back down in the chair.

"What the...?" Maybe two pages had stuck together?

She tapped her finger on the desk, "Okay...is she saying that she shot him and left him to die?" She looped a long red curl around her finger. "Or could she have done something to keep him from being killed?"

"A-*hem.*"

As Rachael shot up at the sound of the deep male voice, her chair fell over making a huge banging noise. Here she was, caught lounging on an antique chair reading someone else's diary.

"I'm sorry..." She picked up the chair, turned and stopped short. "You, it's you... I mean him." She pointed to the desk.

He filled the doorway, his smoky grey eyes fastened on her, his thick brown hair falling across his brow and the well-trimmed beard framing a sly smile. His eyes sparkled with humor as he admired the shock that he had caused on her face.

Kayla was right, this damn place was haunted, and he was the most handsome ghost that Rachael had ever seen, not that she had many to compare him with. This is what she had wished for this morning—his ghost roaming the house during the day. Check— wish granted.

"It is indeed. It's me, his greatly removed grandson, Nathaniel." His laugh filled the room. "And, no, of course she didn't shoot him." His voice, deep and resonant, vibrated through her.

"Oh my God, I thought you were his ghost. Scary. You look just like him."

"I'm sorry. I didn't mean to frighten you, but you were so engrossed in Rachael's diary." He rubbed his beard. "I've been away and haven't bothered to shave in a while. Sorry. I guess it does make me look like him."

"You could say that." She walked closer to him, still doubting that he was real. "Her diary was open on the desk. I didn't mean to pry, but the door flew open, the pages flipped and I started reading. Come see this page. Do you know what it means? How do you know she didn't shoot him?"

"Slow down. First, would you like to tell me who you are and why you're in my house?"

He moved closer and his spicy scent engulfed her. He towered over her by at least half a foot. "I'm here for the estate sale? Your sister Sarah said I could look through the house for items I might want to buy... including the house itself. And I'm Rachael."

It was his turn to be surprised. "She's having an estate sale? Buy the house? She's truly something." He shook his head. "Anyway, other than my sister being from another world, this is scary, Rachael and Nathaniel back in this room together. Coincidence?" his right eyebrow rose up. "I think not."

"Stop," she choked out, trying to control her laughing. "Obviously I'm not your Rachael, or didn't you notice the wild red hair?" she answered, fluffing her mane. "If my friend Kayla were here, she would swear you were Lady Rachael's Nathaniel—you would creep her out."

"Hard not to spot the wild red hair and the green smiling eyes. And who do you think I am, my beloved Rachael?"

"Stop it. Now you're creepin' me out."

His laugh filled the room. "What do you have to show me, my beloved Rachael?" He continued to tease her. He stepped up behind her and leaned over her shoulder.

His closeness was disconcerting. "I...She wrote this," she said, pointing to a blank page. Flipping the page back, she saw Lady Rachael's last entry the night she died. "I don't understand? Where did it go?" She flicked forward and all the pages were blank.

"And what do you think you saw?"

"I did see it." She turned quickly bumping his cheek with her nose. "Writing—she wrote something about she should have known better, acted differently. And then I think there was a question—why did she do it or didn't do it?"

"Why did she or didn't she do what?"

"I don't know." She felt like she was in the middle of an Abbott and Costello moment. "That's why I'm asking you, do you know if she shot him?"

"Why do you care?"

"Why don't you?"

"I do, but first I want to know why it's so important to you...Rachael."

When he said her name, it somehow touched her heart, made her feel like she had known him forever even though they had met only minutes ago.

"First, I'm a writer and so Rachael and Nathaniel's story intrigues me. Second, it's a mystery. Don't you want to know what took place that night? Sarah rolled off a bunch of possibilities, but no one seems to know what actually happened. And, whatever it was haunted Rachael until the night she died. She's your family." She could feel his breath on her cheek. "And, lastly, there's some kind of connection between she and I. I felt it when I saw her portrait downstairs. Even your sister said Rachael brought me here for a reason." She turned and placed her hand on his chest as she moved him back.

"Okay," he placed his hand over hers. "First, you have to understand that my sister believes in this cosmic connection stuff, I don't"—he squeezed her hand—"even though Rachael and Nathaniel stand here together in this room. And second,"—he placed his finger against her lips as she started to speak—"finding out what happened that night won't change anything."

The wind forced the doors open again, causing Rachael to jump. The pages of the diary flew and fluttered, finally settling down. Rachael moved to the desk, picked up the book and read the words aloud:

You, Rachael, if you find the truth, things will change. Please.

Then the page went blank.

Rachael turned to question Nathaniel, but he had disappeared.

Chapter Five

"Holy crap, are you kidding me?" Kayla choked on her beer. When she had her breath back, she asked, "That actually happened? You're pulling my leg, trying to get back at me for this morning." She adjusted her glasses and crossed her feet on Rachael's deck railing.

Almost every night during the summer, the two of them would sit and discuss what had happened while they were apart, maybe something interesting in the news or even politics although that topic could become a bit heated.

When they were kids, Kayla would walk along the beach from her parent's small cottage on the bluff to Rachael's parent's place on the Cove. They would cartwheel the summer days away on the beach. During their college days, the two of them roomed together—Rachael studying History and English while Kayla spent her days in the computer lab building strange objects that Rachael never understood. Today, they had apartments around the corner from one another in Boston. In the summer, for as much time as they could, they would seek sanctuary in the Wellfleet cottages where they had grown up.

Kayla's parents had signed over the cottage to her when they made the move to Florida a few years ago. She had a brother, but he had no interest in supporting another house—he had five kids and a wife who was finishing college nights. Kayla's parents would fly up a few times a year and Rachael and Kayla would fly down for the Jewish holidays.

Rachael's parents lived in California, well her mother and stepfather. Her father died when she was eight. When her mother remarried, she overheard her stepfather tell her mother that he had no time for Rachael; he had children of his own to take care of and she was not his responsibility. That day Rachael divorced herself from him. She never understood his attitude but accepted it and protected herself from him. She kept in touch with her mother but never visited. Her mother rarely came east because Rachael made it perfectly clear that she didn't have room for her husband. The Wellfleet cottage had been transferred to Rachael when she graduated from college without her mother's husband knowing anything about it— that was her mother's gift to her. "The cottage is ours and your father would want you to have it," her mother had stated at the lawyer's office.

Rachael sipped her wine, trying to fit the pieces of the day together. "Even I was spooked. You know that joke we made this morning about the captain? Well, I thought my wish had come true—my own captain right in front of me." She could tell that Kayla didn't see the humor in this story one tiny bit. "Funny that Nathaniel couldn't see the writing on the page though, don't you think?" She egged her on. "And I still wonder who wrote those words?"

"Jeez, three seconds, that's it and I would have been gone. I'd have jumped from the balcony if it was the only way to get away from those weirdoes. I told you this morning, it's effing haunted." She took another swig of her beer. "So what else did our ghostly sea captain have to say about all this?"

"Stop with the ghost stuff. He must have thought I was crazy, seeing things that weren't there."

The sun slipped behind Great Island, coating the water with the purples of nightfall.

"Rachael?" a voice came from the darkness at the side of the cottage.

Kayla yelped, hurling her beer bottle toward the voice and tumbling backwards in her chair.

"Ouch. Thanks, that's quite a greeting. Rachael, it's Nathaniel."

"Oh my God, now the ghosts are making house calls." Kayla scrambled up looking for something to protect herself with. "Run, Rachael, run."

Finding no weapons, Kayla stood poised to jump over the deck railing, when Rachael yelled, "Kayla, sit. He's not a ghost. Nathaniel, we're up here on the deck. This is my insane friend, Kayla, who threw the bottle at you." She heard him trip up the stairs and mumble something like "Goddamned stairs."

Making it onto the top step, he said, "Sarah told me where you lived. I hope you don't mind me stopping by like this. I knocked at the front door but no one answered. Cars were out front, so I figured someone was home. I didn't mean to scare everyone. Sorry." He handed Kayla the bottle that she had hurled at him and then shook her hand adding, "See, I'm real."

Kayla eyed him suspiciously, pushing her straight brown hair out of her eyes and retrieving her glasses that had flown off as she fell backwards. "Hi."

"We lost track of time out here and I forgot to switch on the lights. I'm sorry Nathaniel."

Rachael turned to Kayla, "Kayla, this is Nathaniel Rockford Haverford, correct?"

"Almost, I'm the fourth, Kayla, not the original."

"Yea sure, that's what you say." Scowling, she slipped back into her sling chair. "So tell me, if you are blood to all these weirdoes and poltergeists, why couldn't you see the writing that Rachael saw?"

"Kayla," Rachael scolded.

"What? I want to know why he didn't see it and you did."

Rachael turned a questioning look on Nathaniel.

"You actually saw something written on that page? I thought you were joking."

"Oh my God, I was right, the place is haunted. Rachael, stay away… Oh my God, it's true," Kayla's voice carried across the water.

"Shhh… Kayla, stop it, please. I probably just couldn't find the right page. The wind flipped so many of them when the door blew open…."

"The wind? The door blew open again?" Kayla interrupted. "I'm telling you, this is not normal, Rachael. Please don't go back there."

Nathaniel winked at Rachael. "The reason I stopped by was to tell you that whatever you might need for your story, you are welcome to borrow from the house. Just let Sarah or I know what you're taking." Reaching into his pocket, he took out a key and handed it to Rachael. "So you can let yourself into the house in case neither of us is there." He started to leave and then turned, "Sarah told me that you might be interested in buying the house?"

"What?" Kayla stared at Rachael like she was crazy.

Rachael ignored her, "Sarah mentioned that she would like to sell, but didn't think you were ready."

"Thank God," Kayla interjected.

Again, Rachael ignored her.

"I haven't really thought about it, but if you decide you're interested, or even you Kayla, we can talk about it." He stared at Kayla, freezing her in her seat.

"I'll think about it, thank you," Rachael replied.

"Goodnight then, dear ladies. I have to return to Rose Hill; it's my night to haunt." His deep laugh filled the darkness as he disappeared down the stairs and around the corner of the house.

Chapter Six

Rachael bent over Lady Rachael's desk flipping pages in the diary but seeing nothing new. Why didn't Nathaniel see the writing? Her blood runs through his veins. Had he believed her when she had said there was a message? And, if she remembered correctly, Lady Rachael's writing had addressed her by name.

"I need your guidance through this labyrinth, Lady Rachael. Where do I start? You wrote to me before, so you can write again. Give me a hint."

On her way over to Rose Hill, Rachael had called Kayla and made up a story about driving back to Boston for a few days to see a client. She hated to fib, but she didn't need any distractions as she explored Rose Hill. Kayla would only rag on her for being in the house. There was a story buried here and she wanted it.

When she arrived, she had quizzed Sarah about Nathaniel's whereabouts. Her answer was that she hadn't seen him and assumed that he had returned to New York on business. Rachael didn't mention that Nathaniel had given her a key to the house.

All Rachael remembered him saying last night was, "I'll be in touch." Or did he say "when I return?" She had been laughing so hard over his haunting comment and Kayla's screaming that everything else had been background noise. In any case, the house was all hers and she had to get cracking if she had any hope of solving this mystery in the time she had.

"Since neither you nor Nathaniel has helped so far, I'll take it in my own hands and start with your items, Lady Rachael, if you don't mind." She strolled around the bedroom touching the old furniture. "Maybe I'll be lucky and find a clue buried somewhere in this area. What do you think? I'm still waiting for that hint...."

A spot of sun hit a dressing table that stood against the wall across from the bed. Rachael had only seen many of these items in auction books. This table, made of multiple woods including rosewood, was old enough to have belonged to Lady Rachael's mother. She smiled as she saw that there was a red dot on it. It would be hers. Could this be the thing that she would fall in love with... that Lady Rachael had brought her here for?

A fresh, sunny, bright yellow bouquet of roses sat on the top of the dressing table and filled the room with a luscious sweet fragrance. As she leaned over to smell them, she spotted an exquisite antique porcelain backed hand mirror covered with bouquets of purple violets. Another thing that she shared with Lady Rachael, a love of violets. Were these her hints—sunshine, roses and violets?

She could imagine Lady Rachael sitting at this vanity holding up the mirror as she brushed her blond curls, wearing a sapphire blue nightgown that matched her eyes. Her captain watched her from the bed, the heat and intensity of his love showing in his enamored stare. She rose and walked toward him, the spring breeze from the balcony blowing the soft fabric against her skin. He took her in his arms, bringing his lips slowly to hers. They both recognized that in the hours to come, they would create a bond that would link them forever, a child, a son.

Did their story somehow revolve around the mirror? It certainly had seen everything that had happened in this room. Rachael picked it up, turned it over and caught a glimpse of a likeness in the tarnished surface marred by dark spots where the silver backing had worn thin. Blue eyes, not green ones, stared back. Her fingers touched the muted reflection of blond, not red hair, tumbling over creamy, not suntanned skin. The mirror crashed on the table top as it slipped from her hand. Rachael stepped back, not sure what she had just seen.

"Damn you, Kay. This is all your fault, with the ghost talk last night." Rachael felt that she was gathering some of the pieces: the writing in the journal, Lady Rachael's eyes following her from the lonely portrait downstairs, and now, someone else's reflection in the mirror. But how did they fit together? The mirror had to be the key.

She took a deep breath, picked it up and peered down into unmistakable blue eyes that gazed back from a now gleaming, unmarred mirrored surface.

"Oh my God." She stumbled back. "Oh my God…it's her." The mirror tumbled to the floor with a loud clunk.

Rachael needed air, had to process this. She ran to the balcony doors and stopped—where was the piece of wood that had secured them? She threw them open and saw before her a beautifully restored balcony with a perfect view of the harbor. The cool sea air rushed over her hot flushed skin. Closing her eyes, the sounds of the seagulls high above filled her mind.

"Stop it, your imagination is running wild," she whispered. "You're caught up in the history of this house." Her legs wobbled as she struggled to regain her bearings.

A large schooner with dazzling white billowing sails silently made its way into the Harbor heading up Duck Creeke.

Chapter Seven

"M'lady, are you alright? Are you not feeling well?" a female voice from behind Rachael asked. "Please don't catch a chill. The wind is cold off the water today."

Rachael stiffened, afraid to turn. No one else was supposed to be in the house. She pictured Kayla standing behind her, joking, but she knew better.

"I'm fine, thank you. It's stuffy in the room—I needed some fresh air."

"Stuffy? I'm not sure what that means, m'lady. I came to tell you that Carolyn ran down to the wharf as you asked, but she saw no sign of the Captain's ship."

"I'm not your Rachael. I don't understand..." Rachael whispered as she turned and faced a tiny, rosy cheeked young woman in a long yellow cotton gingham dress with a matching ruffled cap covering her raven colored curly hair.

The woman frowned as though not understanding what she had said.

"M'lady, are you sure you are well?" The tiny woman expressed concern as she bent to pick up the mirror from the floor. She wiped the face with her apron and returned it to the vanity.

"I thought I heard a noise up here. But it didn't break, m'lady. No seven years of bad luck. All is good."

No, all was not good—she had already lived through five luckless years, what was another two? She turned from the door and tripped over the hem on her dress. Her hands ran over a soft cotton skirt, not denim jeans. She searched for her cell phone in her pocket—gone. How would she call Kayla? The petite female rushed to help her.

Rachael put up her hand, stopping the tiny maid from touching her.

"I'm fine, really. I just lost my footing." The blood whooshed through her ears while her mind tried to connect the dots. What had just happened?

"I'm sorry, m'lady. Are you sure you're not feeling faint? You are very pale."

"I'm not feeling anything," Rachael responded sharper than she had intended, sensing her legs had turned to wood. A dream, this had to be a dream she kept repeating in her head.

"As I said, m'lady, I sent Carolyn to the wharf as you asked, but she saw no sign of the Captain or his ship. If you are feeling up to it, could you come downstairs, please? I think Maggie has some questions about lunch. And maybe a cup of tea will revive you?" The wisp of a woman turned and hurried out the door, a hand to her mouth, giggling.

"Wait," Rachael called after her, but she had disappeared. Carolyn? Could that be the old woman that Lady Rachael referred to in her diary? And this young woman, could she be Mazie?

She fingered her way past the desk, feeling nauseous and disoriented. Standing in front of the full length oval mirror, she faced the young lady in the painting, her face without color, dressed in a fuchsia cotton floor length dress with a low cut white lace bodice. Blue eyes tinged with the violet of the dress stared back at her. Tousled curly blond hair cascaded over creamy bare shoulders.

"Lady Rachael, this is your work," Rachael stated angrily as she touched the large green opaque opal that hung around her neck and the lace that encircled her breasts. "Somehow you think that transposing me into your body will help me understand what happened two hundred years ago? That I'll discover magically what transpired between you and your Captain by reliving the moment that he died? Why would you want me to do that? Why would you want him to do that?"

She had to remove herself from this nightmare. She rushed back to the desk and flipped open the pages in the diary, looking for a clue as to what had just happened. And then, Lady Rachael's words began to appear:

I told you, you are the only one.

"The only one? What the hell does that mean?" Rachael said out loud. She watched as more words appeared.

You will change the truth....

"I can't change anything. History is history. It will all end the same."

You are stronger than I was. Help me please. Nathaniel will be there.

"Nathaniel was there then... and it ended badly. I can't change the past for you."

You can.... And you will.

The date was April 4th, 1804.

Chapter Eight

Rachael's head ached. She feared that if she hunted Sarah down and asked her what this was all about, she would offer some bazaar story involving the magic of bodily transposition. But she was Rachael's only hope.

She yanked up her skirt, stumbled down the shadowy back stairs, hurried by the kitchen and along the hallway ending up in the dining room. She heard voices calling her name, but she had to find Sarah. She slid across the polished pine floors coming to a stop before the French doors. She spun around.

A few minutes ago, this room smelled old and musty with packed cartons everywhere. Now the crystal chandelier reflected the sunlight like a prism touching everything in the room; the table shone like a mirror. The floors glowed with a newly polished look. The filled boxes had disappeared.

Rachael threw open the sparkling French doors, dashed down the sturdy wooden stairs leading from the veranda to the garden, and snatched up her skirt again as she ran through the garden. Stones dug into the soles of her soft silk slippers. She halted at the beginning of a bright white shell strewn path in front of a sun dial. It read noon.

The air smelled of freshly turned dirt mixed with a tinge of salt air and the scent of early lilacs. A gazing ball stood at the other end of the pathway shimmering with swirls of purple, blue and green. The entire area overflowed with early spring tulips and daffodils with a backdrop of flowering forsythia and quince bushes.

Rachael shaded her eyes, searching for any movement past the budding rose bushes. Where was Sarah?

There was no wheelbarrow and no one in the garden but her.

"Someone help me," Rachael called. "Please, someone wake me up."

"Rachael? Are you hurt?"

Rachael froze, afraid to turn. No one knew she was here. His tone held such concern. Was Nathaniel trying to fool her again? Was he part of this prank with Sarah, hoping to scare her away?

"Rachael, please? Why do you not answer?"

She turned into the sun, ready to confront him. Shading her eyes, she saw him standing there, a tall, broad shouldered form at the bottom of the veranda stairs. The shadows hid his face, but did it make a difference? He could easily pass for the infamous sea captain.

Rachael tried to speak, but no words came. *Wake up. Wake up*, she repeated in her mind.

"I see that I can still take your breath away."

The emotion in his voice touched her deeply.

"I have missed you all these months at sea. I had hoped that when I arrived home, you would fly into my arms," he said, walking toward her, carrying what appeared to be a small bunch of flowers in his hand. "Have I misjudged that you missed me as well?"

At sea? Would Nathaniel plan such an elaborate rouse? Probably not. And if not… could this be Lady Rachael's captain and did he think her to be his Rachael?

Kayla will freak out when she hears about this garden encounter. Rachael had warned her that she would find something that she would love at Rose Hill… had joked that the Captain would be a good match for her. And here he stood. She remained like a statue, mute.

His shadow enfolded her as he halted, towering over her, his face still concealed in darkness.

She accepted the bouquet that he offered—violets. *Oh my God, violets?* She gazed up into chiseled features framed by a closely trimmed beard, grey eyes that caressed her with passion and love.

"My favorite flowers," she whispered, smelling the violets, her eyes locking with his. His smoky gaze made her feel weak, dizzy.

"I know." He grabbed her elbows to steady her. "Are you not well? You look so pale. I heard you call out for help when I first saw you." The smile in his dark grey eyes had turned to concern.

"I'm fine. I caught my shoe on a vine," she lied with what little breath she had while trying to retain her balance. "And then I turned and you surprised me. I never expected to see you here in the garden—today." For once that was the truth. "She said something about Carolyn...." She had totally lost her train of thought.

How could a man, dead for hundreds of years, be standing right in front of her? Yet here he stood, as handsome as his painted likeness—actually, far more handsome in real life and in color. Dressed in a navy velvet jacket with a black vest that showed off his broad shoulders and a bright white tied shirt that set off his suntanned face from being at sea for months, he was a very imposing man. Oh, would she love to snap a photo of him for Kayla. She'll never believe this entire story.

"I told Mazie that I wished to surprise you with my arrival home. Are you not happy to see me? You seem distant, a bit aloof. Have you found someone else's arms more comfortable than mine while I have been away?" His eyes flashed with a hint of anger. "Edwin's maybe?"

Edwin? She hadn't read enough of the diary to learn about all the characters in Lady Rachael's life. She couldn't be discovered as a fraud yet. "No—it's seeing you—for real. Not Edwin, not anyone." He despised Edwin. His hatred was obvious from the way he spoke his name.

"Thoughts of you have haunted me during the entire voyage, Rachael. I drove the ship and crew hard so I could return as quickly as the seas would allow. When I crossed paths with a ship that carried your message, I knew that I had to return immediately. I came as quickly as I could, my love. The crew thought me possessed, and they were correct—I was possessed by you."

"My message?"

"About your father?"

Rachael nodded. Lady Rachael had tried to inform him of her father's death. How sad that it took so long to communicate in this century. And his trip back, how many weeks or months had it taken? How long had she awaited his return, nursing her grief and fearing for herself?

"Your sorrow shows in your eyes. Let's speak of your father later, my love, but now I think it's imperative that I know the answer to my question. You have had much time to think about it and with your current circumstances, your father being gone, I would think you have come to an answer?" He stood like a nervous schoolboy awaiting a test grade.

"Question?" She had to tread carefully, appearing coy, something she wasn't good at.

"You haven't found another, have you?"

He surprised her by cupping her chin in his large, rough hand. Yet, his touch was gentle. The smell of spice engulfed her as it had when Nathaniel was near. Before she could stop herself, she laid a hand on the side of his face, touching his soft beard, convincing herself that he was real. She shook her head slowly, "How could I?"

He moved his cheek sensuously against her fingers, holding her eyes with his. Lowering his head, he brushed her lips tenderly and then softly kissed them. As his lips caressed hers, her thoughts went to Lady Rachael. Did she realize how lucky she was to have this magnificent man in love with her? This captain was a man of experience causing Rachael's blood to run warm from his touch and he knew it. She had warned Kayla that the Captain would be hers.

He broke the spell by speaking, "Your eyes betray your feelings, my love." He smiled, as though satisfied with his effect on her.

"Do they?" she teased him.

"I'm sorry if I embarrass you," he added, continuing to rub her cheek.

"I'm not embarrassed, just surprised." He wasn't sorry at all; in fact, he seemed quite pleased with himself. He knew what effect he had on Lady Rachael. "And your eyes betray your emotions as well." She countered. Had she been too forward? But she needed to put him in his place.

"I like to surprise you."

"I like to be surprised and today has been full of them." His name could be added to the long list of shocking things that had happened so far, the biggest one being in the arms and on the lips of Lady Rachael's sea captain.

"Good ones, I hope." He touched his lips on hers once again.

"Time will tell. What did you ask me before you distracted both of us?" she questioned, placing her hand against his chest, feeling his heart beat. He was definitely real.

"You have changed so, my love, since I've been away. I like it." He hesitated a second as though waiting for her answer. "We've spoken about this many times, but you said you would give me an answer when I returned... so, here I am?"

Since she wasn't totally certain what he had asked, she surmised it was a proposal of marriage. Before she blundered into something that she knew nothing about, she would listen for more clues.

"I know I'm older, and I know I'll be away for long periods of time, leaving you alone. But I promise with all my heart and soul to make you happy. I will give you children to hasten your days and to keep watch over you when I'm not here; there will be servants to tend to you and our family."

A marriage proposal, as Rachael suspected. Why hadn't Lady Rachael shouted her answer from the church steeple when he had originally asked? She would have, although Kayla wouldn't believe that.

"And who will provide love and care for you when you're far from me at sea?" She smiled. It was a pointed question that maybe Lady Rachael wouldn't ask, but she would. After all, it was her dream.

He slid her hand from his cheek to his lips where he kissed the palm, such a simple yet sensual move. "I'll never seek another, you know that."

She almost believed that he would be faithful to her. "You would break my heart if you took another."

"You surprise me, Rachael, stating your feelings so candidly. How you have changed."

"When I give my heart, it's forever. I would expect nothing less from you."

"I will never disappoint you, never. You are my one and only love, the one who haunts my thoughts day and night. I became your captive the very first time I laid eyes on you. Do you remember that day?"

He slid her hand across his lips again sending shivers through her entire body.

"I do," she lied. She remembered the meeting with his descendent Nathaniel and how she felt when she first saw him. He had a presence like this man, tall and dark with the smell of spice surrounding him. His smoky grey eyes flecked with gold were intoxicating like his ancestor.

"Tell me how you felt," she whispered, desiring to hear how Lady Rachael had cast her spell over this gentle giant. His laugh vibrated through her. She caught him off guard. His smile lit up his face. Every woman in town must suffer from the vapors when he passes by, yet he had chosen Lady Rachael. Why?

"You want me to beg, to bare my soul to you once again." His eyes crinkled at the edges. His skin reflected the glow of days in the sun and salt air.

"I desire only to see into your heart." She stood on tiptoes to kiss him. How odd it felt to be so tiny. She was taking advantage of this dream—his lips were too soft, gentle and too real. She prayed that she would never wake up if this was a dream. It had to be, didn't it? Yet Lady Rachael's words echoed through her head: "You are stronger than I was. Help me please. Nathaniel will be there."

"You are bewitching me anew." He interrupted her thoughts, his words caressing her.

"Rachael, you're so different. I can't explain it, but you're unlike the young woman I left behind."

"Am I? Maybe I've matured, grown up these last few years since you've been away. But tell me again how you felt when we first met."

"Come. I'll take you out of the sun. Let's sit on the veranda for a while." Guiding her by the elbow, he led her to a wooden swing. He placed his arm behind her and fingered her neck in a very possessive, intimate way.

She shivered.

"Are you chilled so quickly? Are you sure you are well?" He removed his jacket and draped it around her shoulders, enveloping her in the warmth from his body.

"I'm fine. You have conquered my well known frostiness by wrapping me in your tenderness and love— and your jacket," she joked. "Please, tell me how I cast this magical spell over you and then we can move inside to the parlor."

"Persistent, aren't you? Haven't you heard me bare my soul enough?" He raised his right eyebrow.

Sarah's brother had the same eyebrow quirk.

"Never. I will never grow tired of you telling me how I bewitched you. Please, tell me again."

"Was it three or four years ago?"

Was he trying to trap her? She shrugged her shoulders as though she couldn't remember, as though it wasn't important to her.

"This is your story, not mine."

"It was four years ago an early spring day like today as I recall." He pulled his jacket tighter around her, moving his fingers to the tendrils around her face. "You were young then, far too young for me. Maybe you still are?" he questioned.

"Tell me this tale of yours." She enjoyed this interplay with him.

"My crew and I had secured the ship and I was heading down the plank. Flinging my sea bag onto the wharf as I always do, it flew by you, landing at Mazie's feet. You let out such a scream. I froze thinking that I had killed your lady servant or worse, hurt you. I know you still think I threw it intentionally near you so we could meet, but I didn't. I was careless and could have hurt you."

Dear, sweet Mazie—Lady Rachael had written affectionately about her. She had stayed by her side until she herself had died. Loving and loyal to each other.

He squeezed her hand. The swing moved slightly. He worshiped his Rachael. He was unafraid to say to the woman that he loved the words that most men would never speak. Although Vince had had his moments with his Lizzy Brown quotes. She smiled.

"You waited for me at the bottom of the ramp, hands on your hips, your long blonde hair blowing in the sea breeze, tapping your foot. What a tongue-lashing you gave me for being so careless, so thoughtless. I apologized over and over again, but you would hear none of it. When you looked up at me, those huge crystal blue eyes on fire, I knew at that moment there would never be another woman for me. I had searched for you my entire life—a strong, caring, independent woman who spoke her mind." He searched her eyes for something.

She looked down.

"My crew teased me mercilessly for standing there and allowing a tiny slip of a woman to berate me as you did. They didn't know that you had mesmerized me and I wanted your rant to go on forever. When you finished, you turned and strode off, head held high with a determined walk and Mazie by your side. My heart sank. I had no idea who you were or where you lived. What my search uncovered was that every young man within a hundred miles pursued you. When I called on you a few days later, I did so on the pretense of apologizing to you again. I wasn't about to admit to myself or to you that it was your face and those striking ocean colored eyes that had brought me to your door."

She smiled, tightening her grasp on his large powerful hand. "What you never knew was how much I wished to see you again as well. I sent Mazie on an errand to discover the name of the very tall handsome captain with the stormy grey eyes. I behaved poorly, like a badly spoiled young girl and I wanted to apologize to you. When Mazie returned from her errand, she told me of the many tales that followed you, my handsome captain. And, there wasn't a woman in town, young or old, who didn't know who you were except for me. When you appeared at my door, a bouquet of violets in your hand as today, you stole my heart for good."

His thumb sensuously rubbed her palm.

"I've waited for you to say those words for years, but you never said anything. Why? You left me not knowing where I stood."

"It's inappropriate for a woman to voice her feelings before the man expresses his, true?" She presumed that women said nothing of their wants and desires in this century. She had to watch her step.

"I only wish I had known." He appeared to be lost in his own thoughts then continued, staring into her eyes. "I wanted you to feel something for me, but you appeared so aloof when I was around. You seem so different today. I have to wonder why?"

"Maybe, as I said, I have matured during your absence? A lot has happened since I saw you last." Things like she had conversed with his Rachael, met Nathaniel's grandson cubed, as Kayla liked to call him, and now sat in the nineteenth century, wearing ridiculous clothes, with the most intriguing man she had ever met.

"I know. You have changed, more grown up, maybe. But I sense something else has happened."

She turned away, not wishing to be found out as an imposter yet.

"Tell me what bothers you. I love you, Rachael. You can trust me."

She turned, placing her fingers over his mouth and shook her head, feeling tears coming.

"Are you having second thoughts? Are you afraid that because I'm much older than you that you will live a long time alone after I'm gone?"

She shook her head. "No, please…no talk of loss today. I've had enough sadness this last year." She couldn't think of him not being here, not today when he had just invaded her life. Was he thirty or thirty-five, and she— twenty or twenty-five years old? They could have many happy years together. How quickly it had become she and he. She grasped his hand tightly as though he might escape from her. He would not leave her, not yet.

He leaned in and kissed her softly, "I'm sorry, my beauty."

Caressing his face, she continued, "You must have known that I had feelings for you, but I had obligations that came before my own happiness. It wasn't that I didn't love you." She had no idea where all this information came from. Obligations? Was she somehow channeling Lady Rachael's thoughts? Was she orchestrating all this?

Rachael didn't want Nathaniel to die and she would do what she could to keep him alive, but history wasn't on her side. And realistically, if he didn't die, she would be living in the twenty-first century while he existed here in the nineteenth.

"I know that you had many things to tend to, not the least of which was your ailing father. Your message about his death caught up with me on my way back from Ireland. I'm sorry, I liked your father. He was a fair and honest man." He stopped for a few seconds, a sadness crossing his face.

It must have taken him months to sail across the Atlantic once he had read her note. His toughness was mental as well as physical.

"You are thinner—the sorrow has taken its toll."

"I grieve for him still. The last year has lessened the hurt a little. I remember vividly how he suffered at the end and how I could do nothing to relieve his pain. I even brought doctors here from Boston to see to him, but there was nothing that any of them could do." Her eyes filled with tears for this father that she never knew.

He pulled her close, his head resting on hers. "I'm so sorry that I'm making you relive those sad times. You were always an exemplary daughter. He loved you so, Rachael. I have no doubt that you tended to him with every ounce of care and love that you possessed. I only wish I had been here to make it easier for you. When I heard of his death, I feared that Philip would evict you from this house and Edwin would try to comfort you in my absence."

"Edwin?" She scoffed. "He conspires even now with my brother Philip. After you sailed, Father tried to match me with local eligible men, including Edwin. He became more frantic to find a suitable husband for me when he realized his end was near. He feared that if I was left alone without a protector, I would be taken advantage of. Luckily, through his friends, he heard of Edwin's cruel streak toward women. Father banned him from the house. I knew Edwin lurked in the shadows, waiting for Father to die." Rachael felt a chill run through her as she thought of this young woman alone among such predators. "And Edwin's as old as my father." All of this poured out of her as though it were her story. Lady Rachael somehow provided the information that she needed.

"And me? I'm young?" he questioned, tipping her head so she faced him.

"You are younger and far more handsome and caring than any of the men that came to call on me." She laughed. "And besides, I had already given my heart away. They wasted their time." She squeezed his hand harder.

He sat silently for a few minutes.

"What are you thinking?"

"I'm afraid that with your father gone, Edwin will make a case for easing your brother's burden by caring for you. I know Edwin's kind all too well. And Philip's no better, I'm sad to say."

"Edwin has already spoken to Philip and Philip came to see me. He tried to present a case about how Edwin would take care of me and he could live in Rose Hill and take Father's place." She caressed his face again, feeling so many emotions for this man, this stranger. "I told them both that my heart had already been given away and there was nothing either of them could do to change my mind. I don't think they took me seriously."

They sat and talked as though they had known each other forever.

"Your father was a good man. All he wanted to do was to ensure that you were well taken care of." He hushed her as she started to protest. "Your father and I spoke before I sailed. He voiced a fear that he wouldn't live long enough to see you married—that he would be gone before I returned. He thought Edwin could provide a better material life for you than I could. I told him the rumors I had heard about Edwin's character, of his brutality with women. He asked for proof. I had none. I didn't want to see you end up in Edwin's cruel grasp because your father desired to marry you off." He traced her lips with his thumbs.

"I told him that I loved you, Rachael, and if you hadn't fallen in love with someone else before I returned, I would ask you to marry me, again. The extent of my holdings made him reconsider me as a son-in-law. He thought you too young to be betrothed to me before I left, but he was afraid for you—for you being alone, unprotected after he was gone. He asked that if word reached me of his death, that I would return immediately and marry you. I gladly made that promise."

As he wiped her tears away, she thought of her own father who had been a good and gentle man. He also hadn't lived to see her married, to walk her down the aisle. Her sobs came from a hurt of her own, from deep inside.

He pulled her close. "I'm sorry. I didn't want to bring all this up again, my love. I know that it hurts you so." He kissed her harder this time. She wound her arms around his neck as he awakened feelings that she hadn't experienced in a long time—a yearning, a need, and a desire to belong to someone. She pushed away the thoughts that he belonged to someone else. For now, this man was hers.

"I'm so glad that you are back—I needed you so much." She inhaled the smell of spice and locked it away in her mind for another day, a day when she would relive this dream, when the smell of spice would bring up a vision of this handsome captain.

He pulled away. "I don't mean to inflict my desires on you like this. I'm sorry if I go too far and embarrass you by my forward show of emotions. You have become so intoxicating to me."

"Please don't apologize for kissing me. I am as much at fault as you are," she whispered in his ear, "Ask me."

The warmth of his smile froze time. "You are a vixen, my love."

"Ask me," she repeated, tears brimming in her eyes, "Please ask me." She placed her hands with the violets in her lap.

He searched her eyes and then rose and dropped to one knee in front of her. She pushed back his thick brown hair from his forehead, the silkiness of it sliding between her fingers. He looked like any other young man proposing. But he wasn't—he was a dream, not real and not hers.

Putting her violets on the swing, he took her hands in his, and kissed them. "I'm asking you to be my wife. I'm asking you to marry me, Rachael."

He waited for an answer, but she couldn't speak. She savored the moment, hoarding it in her heart, knowing that would be all that she would have when she awoke.

"I'll build onto my house in the village if it's not large enough for us. You know that you'll never want for anything. I'll make you happy, I promise you that." He watched her and waited for her answer.

"You are a good and kind man, Nathaniel, but I will remain here." His proposal brought back memories of Vince at the airport. But this time she was older and wiser and this man—he made her feel something that she had never experienced before. Even if he didn't exist, she would cherish this moment and him forever. Kayla will never believe that he had actually proposed to her.

He pulled away from her, concern in his eyes. "Are you turning me down? Have I imagined a life with you in vain?"

"No... oh no. Yes, I'll marry you, but I'd like to stay here at Rose Hill."

"Are you sure?"

"Am I sure I will marry you or sure I want to stay here?" she joked, clasping his face in her hands, kissing him on the nose.

He laughed. "Both."

"I'm very sure, on both accounts."

He reached into his waistcoat pocket and removed a small blue velvet box. She had seen a box like this in Lady Rachael's bedroom upstairs in the desk drawer next to his likeness this morning, but she hadn't opened it.

Offering it to her, he asked, "Will you accept this as your betrothal ring?"

She sat paralyzed. "Place it on my finger, please? It will remain there until the day I breathe my last."

He looked up at her, a curious look on his face and love filling his eyes. He unfastened the box and lifted out a blindingly beautiful blue square diamond solitaire, with sapphire baguettes on each side.

"I will love you, Rachael Johnston, wherever I am, until I take my dying breath. You're the love of my life. No matter what happens, remember that and know that I'll return to you. You belong to me and only me forever, never forget that." He slid the white gold band up her tiny finger while looking into her eyes. "I love you, Rachael."

A flash of sadness crossed his face. She wondered if there was more meaning to his words than the obvious. She knew how this love story ended and maybe he did too. Could that be possible? Could Lady Rachael have brought him back to relive his death as well?

She fumbled for words. "Where...?"

"I searched the world for a stone that would be perfect for you—India offered this flawless one. The transparent blue color reminded me of your eyes. The ring was crafted in the hopes that you might accept my proposal. Well?" he asked.

"It's the most beautiful ring I've ever seen." And she meant that as she held her left hand out in front of her. And he—she had no words to describe him. He thought of her—Lady Rachael—even when he was half a world away. His love for her ran very deep, very deep indeed. When she wrote their story, she would tell their descendants that there was no doubt that they loved each other as much as any couple could. It was truly a beautifully tragic love story.

"Even if you had no ring to offer, I would still be betrothed to you today." Now she spoke like him. She leaned in and kissed him.

He responded by lifting her up, wrapping her in his bearlike arms, and swinging her around, kissing her gently. He nuzzled her and laughed. He acted so much like her Vince after he had proposed to her at the airport. How could she have fallen in love with a man that she had known for only a few hours and who wasn't even real? A man who had been dead for hundreds of years? She wrapped her arms tightly around his neck. How would she compare other men to him? He would sadly be dead hundreds of years when she awoke….

Placing her down in front of him, he asked, "You look so sad. Are you sure you want to remain here? Maybe there are too many bad memories?"

"Not sad, just realistic."

"Realistic? You, my Rachael? About what?"

Maybe that was not a term commonly used, or maybe his Rachael was much too spoiled to be realistic.

"I think about us. Things can happen."

"What kinds of things are you thinking of, my love?" His eyes flashed with gold flecks once again as they watched her closely.

"Just me being silly, I guess." She looked away not wanting the building tears to alarm him. "When you are at sea, I'll be far more comfortable here. I have the servants that have been around me for years. Yes, the answer is yes. Will you be comfortable living here? We could live in your house when you are home?" She asked these questions not knowing if women of this era worried about the comfort of their man or if the choice that she had just voiced was considered improper.

"I would be content living anywhere as long as you are by my side. I love you, Rachael, to the very depths of my soul."

How she would mourn the loss of this man. "Say my married name."

"What do you mean?" he questioned, surprised by her request.

"I want to hear you call me by my married name."

"Rachael Johnston, you will become Mistress Rachael Johnston Haverford, wife of Captain Nathaniel Rockford Haverford—that will be you, my love."

"It rather fits me, don't you think," she giggled, surprising herself since it was not something she had done since she was a teenager.

"A rather big name for such a tiny woman." He lifted her up into his arms.

"I'll live up to it, I promise you."

The maid who had found her in the bedroom earlier interrupted, "I'm sorry, m'lady, but will Captain Nathaniel be having dinner with us?"

Rachael looked to Nathaniel for his answer as he placed her down on the floor of the veranda.

"I will Mazie, but I'll not be here until around eight. I need to pick up something off the ship. Is that too late, my love?" He rubbed her arms inside his jacket. For some reason, he made it seem like such an intimate gesture.

Mazie laughed nervously. She was younger than Rachael and very impressionable, but had such love for her mistress. She assumed Rachael had returned that love as well. It was a strange dynamic for her to understand.

"Whenever you arrive, it will be perfect." She kissed him hard, even though Mazie still remained in the doorway. She didn't want any regrets after he left should she wake up alone in her empty bed.

"I love you with my entire heart, Nathaniel Rockford Haverford."

He kissed her forehead, a curious look in his eyes. She slipped off his jacket and helped him on with it.

"I'll see you later, my love?" He turned as he reached the French doors, staring, as though capturing her in his mind as well. He spoke to Mazie and they both slipped away.

Chapter Nine

After Nathaniel left to return to his ship, Rachael remained on the swing. It was twilight and the lingering pinks and purples washed across the harbor. She scanned the garden—everything seemed to be coming to life. The spring bushes were budding, the perennials pushed up through the warming earth, and even the birds chose loose scraps of grass for their nest building.

She felt warm inside, alive even though she somehow was living in the past. There was a silence and solitude here that she didn't have in her life. Time passed slowly with few interruptions.

As she lifted her left hand, the sunset colors reflected off her stunning newly bestowed ring. She questioned how she had become this mysterious man's love? No matter how and no matter why, she was Rachael Johnston, the betrothed of Nathaniel Rockford Haverford, sea captain extraordinaire.

"Lady Rachael, why are you doing this?" she whispered. "Nathaniel's so tempting. Why are you allowing me to fall in love with him?" She fingered the ring, remembering how Vince's diamond had felt on this same finger. She didn't want to fall in love again—it hurt too much. "You must have heard me say I would try and open my heart again—but why Nathaniel? I'll wake up and he'll be gone... dead hundreds of years. Are you that selfish that you would hurt me this way?"

"M'lady? Were you talking to someone?"

Mazie startled her. "No, just to myself, Mazie. I'll probably be doing a lot of that from now on. It's such a beautiful evening. I hate to think of going inside."

"It is, for sure, m'lady. But you have been sitting out here for quite some time. You shouldn't catch a chill. The night air is starting to come... please come in. You should rest and then dress for dinner."

Rachael nodded and reluctantly rose from the swing. She followed Mazie into the kitchen, wondering how Lady Rachael had found such an attentive maid like this tiny young woman. The kitchen was abuzz as they entered.

"Mazie, could you please put this bouquet in water for me?"

Mazie accepted the flowers, opened a cabinet and pulled down a sparkling cut glass vase from the upper shelf.

Rachael had seen that exact vase on the kitchen counter when she walked to the stairs earlier during the estate sale; it had been lying on its side, dusty and cracked with a red dot on it. She would buy it.

"They are lovely, m'lady. Captain Nathaniel never forgets to bring you violets."

Giggles and chattering continued.

"Can I ask what all this noise is about? It's not enough that you all conspire to have Nathaniel scare the life out of me in the garden? Now what?" As if she didn't know. Mazie had a big mouth.

"Oh, m'lady," Mazie replied, arranging the flowers in the short stout container. "We are so happy for you. You have had such a hard year and now the Captain is back and …."

"And what?" Rachael teased, a bit of lightness in her words and a smile on her face. She was beginning to understand the people who surrounded and loved Lady Rachael.

"We hope that we will be planning a wedding soon, m'lady."

Rachael held out her hand, staring at her magnificent ring, "Yes, we definitely will be." She couldn't wait to make Kayla eat all her words about Rose Hill and the good Captain; she had been correct, the Captain was perfect for her.

The young maids danced around the kitchen, clapping, squealing, and linking arms, unable to take their eyes off the ring.

"Alright, alright," Rachael scolded as they twirled her around with them. "You have a dinner to prepare for tonight and I have to change. Nathaniel will be back soon." She couldn't wipe the smile off her face. How quickly one could adjust to someone else's life.

"M'lady?"

"Yes, Mazie?" And how well she had adapted to being addressed as "m'lady." She might have Kayla address her like that when she returned.

"We're all so very happy for you and the Captain. We know that the Captain will keep you safe from harm."

Her words froze Rachael. Mazie knew exactly what had been happening before she arrived. Could she find out what that was without alerting her that she wasn't Lady Rachael?

"Harm?" she asked innocently, knowing that she had to be aware of any threats to herself and Nathaniel. "Not sure we are in harm's way?" She looked directly at Mazie. She might be able to change history if only in her dream.

Mazie eyed her strangely and then continued, "From Sir Edwin? He's not a nice man, m'lady. He will not be happy when he hears the news of your upcoming marriage to Captain Nathaniel." How cute that she continually addressed Nathaniel as "Captain Nathaniel."

"We won't think of him tonight—let's celebrate my betrothal." She loved that word—it seemed to convey so much more than an engagement.

"Will Master Philip be coming for dinner?"

"Master Philip? Why him?" Again she hoped that Lady Rachael would provide her with insight into her brother. Mazie's question held a touch of disdain.

Once again Mazie cast a questioning look at her mistress. "I thought you might like your brother and his wife here so the Captain can tell him of the upcoming wedding himself." Mazie turned away, having provided the clue that Rachael needed.

"Not tonight Mazie—I want this night to be for the Captain and myself alone." She wanted to thank Mazie but knew she couldn't. She had become very possessive already of the Captain, her Captain.

"Lady Rachael, beware," Rachael whispered as she headed up the stairs to change for dinner. "Your plan may backfire. I might save him and keep him for myself."

Chapter Ten

Once in the bedroom, Rachael passed by the vanity without stopping. The hand mirror lay face down. It had functioned as the portal into the nineteenth century and she had no doubt that it had the power to send her back to the twenty-first. Given a choice, she'd stay here, remain Lady Rachael, and have Nathaniel in her life for as long as she could.

But where was the other Rachael these days—had she taken over her life? If so, she must be very disappointed. Kayla would make her as a fake in two seconds and have the police out searching for the real Rachael. If only she had her phone—one selfie of her with Nathaniel and Kayla would go crazy. Although, now that she thought about it, Kayla wouldn't even know that it was her.

"I'm sorry Lady Rachael, but I'm not returning today." She had to go home sooner or later, but she fancied the company of her sexy sea captain a little bit longer.

Standing in front of the large oval floor mirror, Rachael adjusted the soft blue tulle empire dress that she had chosen from the closet. It fell softly off her shoulders, with the fluffy see-through clouds of material reaching to her elbows. She had chosen to wear her hair up tonight in a more formal look.

Lady Rachael's outfits exposed too much cleavage for Rachael's taste with necklines that were provocative, not what she would have chosen to wear to dinner. She would have appeared in her oversized Tee-shirt and jeans. How weird it felt to be captured between two worlds—and know it.

Walking out on to the balcony, she caught the last bit of twilight reflected off the white billowing sails of a large schooner entering the Harbor. Someone's captain was returning home, she mused.

Returning to the desk, Rachael wanted to see if maybe more words of wisdom might have appeared for her. It seemed to be the only way that Lady Rachael could communicate with her other than filling her head with information when she needed it.

The diary did indeed contain a new message.

Be very careful… they will try to kidnap you.

"How do you do this?" Rachael asked aloud. "You scare the living daylights out of me every time you write something. Tell me, who's going to try? How can I use this information if you only give me bits and pieces? I can't warn Nathaniel because I don't know what's going to happen." All of a sudden, she heard a commotion outside on the driveway below.

She hid in the shadows of the balcony. A well-dressed older man exited from a carriage in front of the house. Could this be Edwin? He adjusted his hat and carried a walking stick with a head that reflected the lingering twilight. His posture said arrogant, wealthy and paunchy.

Hurrying down the stairs and into the hallway, Rachael heard a disturbance at the front door. "Show time," she whispered.

"Please, Sir Edwin, m'lady is not available."

"Mazie, is there a problem?" Rachael asked, coming up behind her.

"Sir Edwin was asking to see you. I told him you were resting."

"I will speak to him in the front parlor, Mazie. You continue with dinner please and have Carolyn bring us some tea."

"Yes, m'lady. If you need me, please pull the bell cord." Mazie backed up, giving Edwin a warning look. "Would you like me to take your hat and cane?" Mazie asked halfheartedly.

"No. I'll keep them with me. My business will not take long." He was condescending and rude.

"Thank you Mazie. Edwin, please come into the parlor."

As they entered the room, Rachael couldn't believe how cozy the room seemed. The drapes, freshly washed and pulled back, provided a perfect view of the garden through sparkling windows. A mounted three piece silver framed mirror sat on the mantle of the stately grey marble fireplace reflecting the pinks and purples of the sunset; a peach velvet couch faced the hearth.

She slid her ring off and dropped it in her skirt pocket. "It's nice to see you, Edwin. Is there something in particular that brings you to my home tonight?" She dove right into why this obnoxious little man stood here. She knew the comment about her home would set him off and maybe force him to show his true colors.

Edwin's eyes wandered to her breasts, his breathing quickening. "I visited your brother earlier today and he thought I should stop by and see how you were handling your father's estate. It's a large responsibility for such a young, inexperienced woman." He flashed a lascivious smile.

Men like Edwin capitalized on the fact that a woman in Lady Rachael's situation was shielded from predators for only a year after the death of their protector. What Edwin didn't know was that Rachael would make sure that he didn't manhandle and take advantage of Lady Rachael. Had he seen Nathaniel's ship in the harbor?

"I'm doing very well, Edwin." She fussed with the lace over her breasts, trying to cover a bit more of the bare skin.

"You do appear well, Rachael. I don't think I've ever seen you looking so luscious," he said, almost drooling.

"Edwin, as nice as that is to hear, is there a reason for you being here?" She was losing patience with this dirty old man.

"Well, since you are carrying such huge obligations now, Philip and I assume that you are finding it stressful to handle everything your father left you. We are worried about you, living in this big house by yourself, taking care of all these tasks." His cane caught the reflection of the candles as he waved it around. "You need a man to help you with them."

How transparent could he be? Did comments like his really work in the nineteenth century?

Edwin paused while the maid placed the tea on the table in front of the couch. Carolyn poured as Rachael showed Edwin to the sofa. He dropped his hat and cane on the pillow as he waited to speak.

"Is there anything else, m'lady?"

"This is perfect, thank you, Carolyn." *Another faithful maid,* Rachael thought. She could trust these women implicitly.

Carolyn bowed slightly and backed out of the room.

"I'm not sure I understand, Edwin," Rachael played along.

"Well, a group of women living together without a man in the house are prey to all kinds of ruffians. They could break in and have their way with any of you."

Rachael stared over the rim of her cup, sipped her tea, and waited for him to continue with his chauvinistic views. The only ruffian who would try to have his way with her would be him.

He cleared his throat, "We, well, Philip has decided that you should wed."

Rachael almost choked on her tea.

"Are you alright?"

She bit her tongue to keep from screaming at him. She nodded, placed the tea cup and saucer down on the table, and fingered the large blue diamond inside her pocket. She couldn't wait for the perfect time to spring it on him.

"You do agree that it would be best, Rachael, don't you?" His anger rose with the loudness of his voice at her silence. The redness in his cheeks increased.

"I do." Again, her response was curt.

His eyes wandered back down to her breasts. "I was thinking May." His tongue darted across his thin, dry lips. "Could you be ready by then?"

"May? Ready for what? You are confusing me, Edwin." She played the ignorant, innocent young woman while knowing exactly where this conversation was going.

He rose and grabbed her by the arms, trying to pull her to her feet.

His fingers embedded themselves in her soft skin bruising her. "Ouch. Stop it. What are you doing, Edwin? You're hurting me."

He yanked her close holding her wrists tightly, attempting to plant a wet kiss on her mouth. Rachael anticipated his move and turned her cheek to him. She shuddered as he slobbered on her skin. Tearing from his grasp, she landed a loud smack on his face. This unexpected consequence of his attempted kiss caused even more anger to flare in his eyes.

"You ungrateful witch," he hissed, grabbing her shoulders and shaking her. "I was just sealing our betrothal with a kiss. You will marry me. I'll have my way with you and you will be my wife. And I will tend to your father's business." He grabbed for her breasts.

"Stop. Betrothal? How dare you, you arrogant, misguided, overbearing old man! Marry you? I never agreed. What a laugh." She slapped his hands away, wiping the salvia from her left cheek with the back of her hand. "You're no gentleman, Edwin. Please leave my home right now."

He took a threatening step toward her as Rachael raised her hand to block him. "Leave now and don't return. Ever. Do you understand?" Her anger flared at his inability to grasp what she said.

"Philip and I have decided that you will marry me in May. And you will be my dutiful wife, my beauty, and move into my house. Philip will live here at Rose Hill." He straightened his waistcoat as though everything was decided. He had no idea of the rage that boiled inside her.

"Really? It's you who doesn't understand me. Listen closely to my plans, Edwin. I am to marry, but not you." It was time. She slipped on the ring, pulled her hand out of her pocket and waved it in front of him. He flinched, thinking she was about to strike him again. The flash of the diamond stunned him. Inside, Rachael was thrilled at the shock on his face.

"I am already betrothed and plan on remaining in this house, my home, for some time."

The front door opened and closed. *How perfect*, Rachael thought, smiling. It was Nathaniel.

"Betrothed to whom? I don't understand. That's not possible—you did not receive Philip's approval." His cheeks became even blotchier. She hoped that he didn't expire right here. Kayla hadn't said anything about another death in Rose Hill, did she?

"She doesn't need her brother's permission to marry." Nathaniel's frame filled the parlor doorway as his voice permeated the room. "And if you ever touch her again, I swear I'll kill you where you stand. That's a promise." His face was hard and flints of fury flashed in his stormy grey eyes.

"Philip will not like this." Edwin spoke directly to Nathaniel, ignoring Rachael like she wasn't even there. "It's to you that she is promised?" He shook his head. "Philip will not be pleased with this, not at all."

Rachael stepped in front of Nathaniel to gain Edwin's attention and felt Nathaniel's hands caress her shoulders. "Philip has nothing to say about whom I marry or where I live. Rose Hill is my home, left to me by my father, and I will live here for as long as I please. I would appreciate it if you would leave now. You are no longer welcome here, Edwin. My father told you that over a year ago and now I'm informing you again of my wish. You are never to return to Rose Hill."

"This is not over." Edwin bent to pick up his hat and cane from the floor where they had fallen.

Nathaniel shifted around Rachael and stepped in front of Edwin, towering over the older man. "It is over, Edwin. Rachael has accepted my proposal of marriage and we are to be married soon. If you ever come to her home again, I will be forced to take actions I would rather not take. Find another wealthy woman to prey on."

Edwin fell back as though physically struck by Nathaniel's last words. He dared to swing his walking stick at him, but Nathanial blocked it with his arm.

"Do not make me hurt you, Edwin—leave now, while you can."

Edwin pushed Rachael out of his way, muttering. The door slammed behind him.

"Are you alright?" Nathaniel rubbed the red marks on her arms. "I should have taken care of him today. I didn't realize until now that he had hurt you."

Snuggling against his chest, she wound her arms around his back. "I'm fine. He doesn't frighten me." Nathaniel's words, "taken care of him" echoed in her head, his meaning quite clear. Differences were settled physically here and usually ended in the death of one of them.

"He should frighten you, my lovely." He rested his chin on her head. The timbre of his voice vibrated through her. "Edwin's an evil man, Rachael, capable of almost anything. You should never be alone here or anywhere else until you are my wife. He has desired your father's fortune since he died. Now that your year of mourning is complete, he'll make his move. There's nothing that he wouldn't do to have you, even kidnap you from this house or off the street. He's not to be trusted." He rubbed his hands along her back.

"Then we should marry soon." His words and tone concerned her. Kidnapping? That must have been how men took what they wanted with little if any repercussions.

Nathaniel held her away. "When?"

She laughed at his quick response and clasped his face in her hands. "How long before you sail again?" Whatever the date, it would be too soon for her—for Lady Rachael. How would she exist knowing that he would be gone for months, maybe years, maybe never come back? And would she be here when he returned?

"Probably six months, maybe seven. You know how this goes—I have to fill the ship with items I can trade and then I have to plan a profitable trip. I assume you want to wed before I set out to sea again?"

"Yes, definitely. If we don't, you will be gone another year, maybe longer. Too long with all these threats against you and me—yes, now."

"I love you, Rachael. I would take you as my wife tomorrow if you could be ready."

"I doubt I could plan a wedding by tomorrow," she caressed his lips with a slow, sweet, soft kiss. He intoxicated her. His soft gentle kiss would remain on her lips long after she awoke from this dream.

"How soon?" he whispered. His words made her want to run right out and find a Justice of the Peace.

"A week, maybe two?" He made it hard to concentrate. Could she buy a dress and plan a wedding in that amount of time?

"Wait here; I have a surprise for you." He went to the hallway where she heard whispers and giggles.

Standing at the windows, Rachael wondered how long it would be before she would have to leave. How could she return to her drab life without him? In less than one day, she had fallen in love with this man. He was good and solid and loyal and loving. Maybe she was building on the feelings of Lady Rachael, but whatever it was that she felt, she knew that her life would never be the same. Kayla had her wish – Rachael had opened up her heart only to allow a man to walk in who belonged to someone else, lived in the nineteenth century, and was dead. She might inhabit the body of Lady Rachael, but she had the mind and heart of Rachael Corbet. How long would Lady Rachael allow her to remain in this world knowing that she loved her Captain?

She turned as Nathaniel entered the room carrying a large box wrapped in brown paper. He laid it on the sofa, beside Minerva, the Persian cat who had taken up her usual position now that Edwin had departed. Minerva eyed the package, sniffed it and then, rolled up in a ball with a heavy sigh.

"Are you alright? You look so sad. Was it Edwin's visit?"

"No, not sad. Wistful maybe?" She swiped away a tear from her cheek.

"Are you thinking of your father? Or are there other regrets I should know about?" He closed his arms around her. "Tell me your sorrows and I will make them go away."

"It's nothing. I don't want this time to end." She cupped his bearded face in her hands.

"I won't let our love die, Rachael, you know that."

His words hit her hard. It would die, he would die and she would be alone in a faraway century. "We have no idea what the future holds for either of us. Please, tonight, let's not talk of loss and the time beyond these hours. We have much to celebrate. What have you there?" She pointed to the box.

He hesitated, as though processing what she had said. "I agree, my sweet. Tonight we will make plans for our wedding. When I discovered these items on my travels, I thought that if I was lucky enough to have you agree to be my wife, you might accept them." He stood with his hands behind his back.

"Should I open the box?"

He nodded. "Please."

"I love your surprises." She sat on the couch, making sure not to disturb Minerva, ripped open the paper that held the box together and lifted the top. There rested a bolt of beautiful handmade Irish lace. On her visits to Ireland, she had never seen any like this.

"It's gorgeous." She searched his face. "But why?"

"Since you will be having your wedding dress made, I thought the lace might be a nice adornment— covering…." He fumbled with his words. "There's more."

The portrait of Lady Rachael above the fireplace flashed through her mind. Her bodice had been covered with this cream colored lace. Touching it lovingly, Rachael understood that somehow she was truly linked with Lady Rachael, Rose Hill and their history.

"Keep looking under the lace," he prodded, wanting her to see the rest.

As Rachael lifted the lace, she glimpsed a gorgeous roll of matching silk. She stared at him again, questioning why he would give her such a gift.

"For your wedding gown and our wedding night?" His face flushed, looking down at her as she rubbed the silk against her cheek. "I know it's forward of me to gift you such personal things, but this kind of material could never be found around here or in Boston. I hope that I have not offended you?" He watched for her reaction.

Jumping up, she hugged this very dear, considerate man. "You are a very caring and thoughtful man, Captain Nathaniel Rockford Haverford. You make me so very happy and you could never offend me. You thought of me as you travelled the world." She kissed him gently.

He touched her face, her hair, and held her so tightly that she could hardly breathe.

"I think of you always—with every breath I take. You test my will power today, Rachael." His breath was ragged.

"You test mine as well, my Captain," she whispered in his ear, wishing he would carry her upstairs.

"You are different, showing your emotions and affection. I love you, Rachael. When we part, I will search for you in every corner of the world." His words, said in an ominous tone, sent chills through her.

"I will wait for you, Nathaniel, never doubt that. No matter what distance separates us, my love and thoughts will find you. I wish that we could freeze time tonight." She took his hand in hers. "Come and we will discuss our wedding plans over dinner."

She changed the subject knowing that soon she would have to leave him—but not tonight.

Chapter Eleven

Polished silver candlesticks holding flickering candles adorned the table, casting a romantic glow across the dining room. Rachael and Nathaniel talked, laughed and ate as though they commonly took an evening meal together.

Rachael studied the tough seafaring man across from her and wondered where the pull of the ocean and the strong winds had taken him through the years. What did Lady Rachael know about his most recent voyage?

"I know that you sailed to Ireland and India, but tell me more about the rest of your trip."

He raised a questioning eyebrow, "Usually you are bored to tears when I speak of my journeys?"

"Since I sail my own ships these days, I don't wish to be in competition with you. Maybe I should know more about your routes? Or more importantly, maybe I have a vested interest in where your ship puts in from now on." Rachael had to tread carefully here with him as she was definitely entering into unchartered waters.

"And that would be?"

She flashed her left hand and the blue diamond at him, making him smile oddly. "The Captain is now very much my interest. He should only be entering ports where there are no women or if there are females, he should be sending his men onshore while he stays onboard."

He threw back his head, letting out a low rumbling laugh. "Jealous? You, Rachael? And all this time I thought you took me for granted. How comforting to know that you care," he mocked her.

"Jealous? Me, never. But I'd be a very foolish woman not to be concerned about a man like you. Here in town, in front of me, you are openly pursued." She watched his lips rise in a small knowing smile. Obviously she was correct; there must be many women who would set a trap for this wealthy handsome man.

"Really? And you have noticed all these women falling at my feet?" He played games with his Rachael. "And what of the many suitors who lined up at your door? Your father controlled their advances while he lived, but he has been gone a year. Who kept all those pursuers at bay while I was pining away for you at sea?" he teased her.

"Pining, was it? Hmmm…I wonder if the crew would agree. I bet many an Irish lass or two dreamed of comforting the handsome, lonely sea captain far from home." Now she fastened a questioning look on him.

His dimple appeared through his closely trimmed beard, "And you my love, what young lads comforted you while I fought the storms and demons at sea?"

"You forget that I was in mourning for a year after my father died. I have only recently put away my black weeds. And here you are, snatching me up when I'm at my weakest, before others have a chance."

He studied her with a curious smile. She knew that his Rachael never would have spoken to him as she just had. She enjoyed keeping this confident man off balance.

"I only joke, but I know you had a hard year with your father not here. You have matured so much these last two years that I have been away."

"Have I?" She had to know more about this woman whose body she inhabited. "How?"

"You are more thoughtful and caring, much more self-assured. You are a very capable, level headed woman with a sensuous, teasing side. You cause me to fall even deeper under your spell, my beautiful one."

He reached for her hand, sending a tingle through her body. His Rachael sounded like a spoiled young woman who was doted on by her father.

She caressed his hand. How could she have fallen in love with this stranger? But Nathaniel was no stranger to Rachael. She had to remember that she was only borrowing him.

"Well, in that case, we should marry while you are still enchanted. I won't take any chances," she joked. He had wanted to marry Rachael for years. "What are your thoughts for a wedding?" she asked, finishing up her meal.

"My wish is for you to have the wedding of your dreams."

Rachael had no wedding dreams. The only wedding that she had ever considered was in a hospital room with Vince and that entailed a simple white suit which she never wore and still hung in her closet. As a little girl, she was too busy with softball and hockey to dream about frivolous things like a wedding. She never even owned a Barbie doll. And, now she had to think like Lady Rachael—what did women in this century dream of?

He must have sensed her hesitation as he squeezed her hand. "Are you not prepared to think about a wedding? I thought you would have it all planned out by now. Don't most women?"

"I'm not most women," she responded a bit sharply.

"I'm sorry. I didn't mean to offend you, Rachael. Before I sailed, you spoke of a wedding in the small church on the hill with a garden reception here at Rose Hill? Is that what you still desire?"

"That was before Father died. Now I have no one to give me away. If Philip were a real brother, he would give me away, but instead, there's no one." She spoke the truth because Rachael's own father was dead as well.

"Could we have the ceremony in the garden, under the arbor in the back? I would feel more comfortable walking down the path by myself to meet you." Was there an arbor in the garden? Again, Rachael channeled Lady

Rachael's wishes or more likely those were her plans before Nathaniel died.

"I would marry you on the wharf or on my ship if you chose that." He joked trying to cheer her. "A garden wedding sounds perfect. You will be a most beautiful bride. Now, do you have a date in mind?" He continued with his meal while awaiting her answer.

Mazie appeared at the door, interrupting them, "I'm sorry to intrude on your dinner, m'lady, but Master Philip is asking to speak to you. I had asked him to come at a more convenient time, but he insisted on speaking to you now. I asked him to wait in the sitting room. I'm sorry, m'lady…"

"You had no choice, Mazie. Did you inform him that the Captain was here?"

"No, m'lady, I thought that might be something you would rather do. Would you like me to tell him?" Mazie always wanted to please.

"No, that's fine. I'll talk with him. Thank you. Please hold the special dessert until Philip is gone." She glanced at Nathaniel, seeing the anger rise in him over what Edwin had blurted out earlier about Philip.

"Please finish your meal while it's warm." He started to protest. She held up her hand. "I would ask that you wait here, Nathaniel, until I call for you. I have to handle Philip myself." She stood, walked behind his chair, leaned over and kissed his cheek.

He took her hand and kissed her palm. "I will leave his visit to you, my love—until I hear him raise his voice. Then…"

Chapter Twelve

Rachael raised her skirt and entered into the sitting room. Would she ever adjust to wearing long full skirts? Every day felt like prom night. She smiled, remembering how handsome Vince had looked in his tux as she had greeted him at her door. She had chosen a black straight gown…it might still be in the back of her closet, now that she thought about it. She'd worn her hair pulled up in a braided knot on the top of her head. Vince had undone the braids before the night was over, saying that he loved her long curly hair loose around her face. She had never worn it up again...until tonight. But then, it wasn't really her blond hair, was it? She hadn't been able to move past Vince because everything reminded her of him. Would the same be true when she returned to her twenty-first century life—everything would remind her of Nathaniel?

"Rachael, you certainly took your time coming."

Philip had abruptly broken into her thoughts. Edwin had been found to be dangerous. What would Philip turn out to be?

"Philip, how nice to see you too," Rachael smiled and offered her hand which he immediately dismissed. Well, he was rude. She had her work cut out with this one. He presented yet another of the characters in Lady Rachael's story.

"I wish I could say the same, Rachael." He remained sitting, shoving Minerva off the couch to aggravate his sister. The cat turned on him and hissed. "She's adopted your traits, I see."

"Your manners have truly deteriorated. Mother wouldn't be happy with you. You could at least rise when a lady enters the room."

"A lady? My, haven't we become haughty now that we are an heiress." He sneered.

"Why are you here, Philip? I'd like to return to my dinner before it becomes cold." Her brother was intolerable. He intimidated Lady Rachael by taking on the authoritarian role, but he wouldn't browbeat her, not tonight.

"I'm here to inform you that you will indeed be marrying Edwin this weekend. And you will move your belongings to his house and then, Hannah and I will move here to Rose Hill."

He said "Rose Hill" in a triumphant tone as though everything was settled because he said so. Rachael shook her head. Everything had been settled, but not be to his liking. She would toy with him a while longer.

"Really, Philip? I believe you're mistaken. As I told Edwin earlier, I'm over twenty-one and am free to choose my own husband. And, secondly, if I remember correctly, Father's will states that Rose Hill is mine, not yours."

Philip jumped off the couch, snarling at her because she dared to speak up to him. Rachael shifted back, banging into the dining room door, holding it open with her foot so that Nathaniel could hear the conversation.

Philip frightened her; there was madness in his eyes. He leaned in so close to her face that she could feel his hot, stale breath on her cheek. He hissed between his teeth, "You overindulged little witch. You'll do as I say. Father was stupid, out of his mind leaving anything to a daughter, especially you, a frivolous, spoiled brat. He catered to your every fancy—it was truly disgusting to watch. This should all be mine and it will be." He threw his arms wide, startling her. "You will have nothing but what I dole out to you, do you hear me?" His voice rose.

"Stop threatening me, Philip. It will do you no good. I'm not afraid of you anymore." Her voice was strong and steady, belying how she felt inside. "You need to leave *my* home—now."

He raised his hand to strike her, but Rachael was ready for him. He wouldn't hurt Lady Rachael this time. She struck at him first, a chop across his raised arm. He yelped, falling back, shock in his eyes. The door behind Rachael opened and she tumbled back into a hard-muscled chest.

Silence filled the room as Philip adjusted to the sight of Nathaniel behind her.

Nathaniel's heated stare froze Philip where he stood.

"Rachael, my wife-to-be, has asked you very politely to leave her home, Philip. Considering your actions toward her, I would advise you to go quickly before I become less than charitable. And as a further warning, if you ever raise a hand to her again, if she doesn't maim you, I will." He took a step toward Philip.

Rachael placed her hand on Nathaniel's chest, stopping him. She could feel his rapid heartbeat.

"Philip, Nathaniel and I are betrothed and will marry soon. While he's at sea, I will live here at Rose Hill, my home."

"You are not entitled to this house—I am. Father was sick, out of his mind when he left you his estate. It should have gone to me, his son, not a coddled daughter like you. Marry the good Captain and move out. I won't care. But I'm entitled to the house and father's business."

"Entitled? Why, because you're a male?" Now her temper flared. "You, who couldn't be bothered with your father when he needed you most, you who couldn't make time to say goodbye to a man who had bailed you out of every predicament that you found yourself in—women, money? How could you expect him to entrust his hard earned fortune to the likes of you? You would lose everything that he amassed in his lifetime in six months. He knew you well, Philip; you received exactly what you deserved—one ship. And that was very generous of him. I would have had him leave you nothing." Tears came for a father she never knew and revulsion for a brother she never had. She stood her ground, hands on her hips.

"Please leave now, Philip. I am remaining at Rose Hill and will be marrying Nathaniel. It's not up to you to decide who inherits what—Father did that, whether you like it or not. And I'm old enough to choose my husband."

Nathaniel whispered, "Well said, my love, well said. You never stop surprising me."

She squeezed his hand at her waist.

Philip glared at her, trying to form words as Nathaniel took his arm and escorted him out the door.

"You have upset Rachael enough. You heard her decision. Accept it, Philip or…"

Rachael couldn't hear the rest of the conversation as words were exchanged between Nathaniel and Philip. And then, the front door slammed.

"Well, my beauty, shall we finish our dinner?" Nathaniel offered his arm. "Now you know what I mean about Philip and Edwin being dangerous. And, where did you learn to fight like that, may I ask?"

"An unwed woman has to be able to take care of herself as you can see." She squeezed his arm, lifted her skirt, and headed for the dining room. And Rachael had to take care of Lady Rachael; women were not afforded much respect or choice in this century. Leaning her head against Nathaniel's arm, she smiled, thinking that working out at the gym and attending the self-defense classes had paid off, even here in the nineteenth century.

Chapter Thirteen

Rachael had taken full advantage of Nathaniel's goodnight kiss. Would her role playing come back to haunt her? She had to laugh out loud. "How could it be any worse? You already haunt my dreams."

She would live out this time with no regrets, no would've, should've, or could've as her Dad used to warn. She already had too many in her real life. And what would Vince think of all this? He had set her free that afternoon… squeezed her hand and said goodbye. He and Nathaniel would have gotten along so well. She had closed herself off from life for far too long. She needed to live, really live, not just walk through her days.

She lay on the bed, afraid to fall asleep, fearful that if she did, she would awake in the twenty-first century. She wanted to stay here where life was simple and someone loved her. But her wishes didn't count, she knew that. She hadn't controlled her arrival and probably wouldn't have a say in her departure.

Rachael lit the candle on the bedside table and carried it to the desk, not wanting to waste any more time. Maybe reading more of Lady Rachael's journal would answer the questions that she had about the woman whose life she now lived. She flipped the pages and started to read aloud. It happened to be the day Lady Rachael's father died…

February 15th,
I am alone tonight except for dear Mazie and Carolyn. They hover near trying to make things better for me. But times will never be better. I am an orphan now. Father drew his last breath at sunset. I've sent many

messages to Philip, the last one earlier in the day when I was sure that Father would not make it through the night. Philip of course was too busy to come to say goodbye to his father. Oh how I wished for Father to stay. I am selfish, I know. But he has been my friend and confidante since Mother died and now, now I have no one. Who will protect me from Philip and all the other vultures who pursue me, like Edwin—well, in truth, they pursue Father's wealth, not me. My mourning period provides a year of safety, but what then?

Father lies still and cold in the living room. I sit by his side—weeping for what was. I will miss him at the morning table smiling across from me, at his books working well into the night, dressed in his tall hat as he leaves the house, looking so handsome. I think of all the women who pursued him after Mother died. But he always said, there would never be another to take her place, and there never was. Oh, to have a man love me like that.

In a few hours, I will take Father to be with Mother. He will be happy to join her—he has missed her so much. And, in a strange way, I'm happy for him because his suffering is over. He left me his estate and I promised him before he died that I would make him proud. He spent hours writing his instructions down and then we worked on the books together these last few months. I'm ready to take charge of his shipping business.

Philip tried to force Father to change his will before he died—he was not happy with the terms, but he cannot contest Father's wishes or he loses everything. After Father refused his request, he never returned, not even as Father lay dying. How that had hurt him. Father's last will and testament will not stop Philip from devising a plan to steal Father's wealth, my responsibility now. I hate to say this of my only sibling, but Philip is greedy and has no conscience.

Nathaniel has been on my mind these last few hours as I sit here. I had Mazie send messages to him about Father's death via the ships leaving port. Maybe one of them will cross paths with his vessel. I have been hoping that he would propose marriage again now that I am free. I do love him even though he thinks me a spoiled child. He may have been correct when he left, but these last few months, with Father unable to function, have allowed me to mature and handle the household duties as well as many of the business transactions, learning how to be accepted in a man's world. Not an easy chore for a young woman.

I'm so alone now, Father. I love you and miss you so—already.

I will try to sleep a bit here in the chair. I have a long hard day ahead. It's cold. The fire wanes. The cold reaches my heart. I can't believe that you are truly gone.

Nathaniel—where are you? I need you so much....

Rachael's tears blurred Lady Rachael's last words, words of a woman overwhelmed by grief and sadness. How unique she must have been for her time. Maybe that's why they had bonded and why she had been chosen to come back in time and live in Lady Rachael's body. She flipped through the pages and found the notes for yesterday.

April 4th,

I visited Father and Mother today and left them a bouquet of the first daffodils to bloom here on Rose Hill. Mother loved them so. I reassured Father that all was well and that I have actually increased his holdings this last year. Our new ship will sail next month with a full crew and a new captain. I will christen her "The Rose "and she will head east.

I have not heard from Nathaniel—I watch every day for his ship, sometimes from the balcony, sometimes I walk to the wharf, but never alone. I fear that with my year of

*mourning complete, Philip and Edwin are plotting to take
Father's estate and this house that I love so much from me.*

I am telling you, Rachael—be alert.

The last line jolted her back in the seat. Lady
Rachael had somehow written a warning to her at this
moment. Rachael tightened her robe around her as a cold
wave washed over her. It wasn't only the chill and
dampness of an early spring night—it was the knowledge
that something that she didn't understand was about to
begin.

Rachael picked up the pen... if Lady Rachael could
contact her this way, maybe she could write back to her.

Why, Rachael? What's about to happen?

She held her breath waiting, waiting...a long second
went by and then sentences began to appear letter by letter,
word by word on the page.

*They are coming for you and Nathaniel tonight.
Protect him and yourself, please. You are my only hope.*

Who comes, Rachael?

She waited. Nothing. Rachael wrote again.

Who comes? I need to know what to expect.

She paced. No more words came. She was on her
own. Lady Rachael knew everything—what had happened,
what had been happening and what was going to happen.
But Rachael could only guess. How could she save
Nathaniel if she didn't understand what occurred centuries
ago? Lady Rachael needed to provide more information.

One bad move on Rachael's part and she would be captured and Nathaniel would be killed…again.

As she closed the balcony doors, Rachael heard sounds outside. A broken branch? A whispered word?

"Be alert… they are coming for you and Nathaniel tonight." Lady Rachael's words tumbled through her mind. If only she knew what to expect, how Lady Rachael had responded centuries ago, then maybe she could act differently.

"Lady Rachael, I'm here one day. I don't even know the lay of the land. Please help me…," she whispered as she turned the lock on the balcony doors

The written warning had been clear—whatever it was would happen soon—they were coming for her and probably stood below her balcony already. She had to warn Nathaniel. She ran to the bedroom door, but realized that she couldn't go out dressed in her robe and nightgown. She placed the candle holder on the floor as she rummaged through Lady Rachael's closet—dresses and more flouncy dresses. Didn't she own anything else? Yanking the cluster of gowns aside, she went down on hands and knees and felt around. Rachael always hid old clothes in the back of her closet; maybe her namesake did the same. Her hands hit pieces of clothing folded on the floor. She smiled—Lady Rachael was indeed like her. She pulled out gardening clothes with a man's hat on top. She assumed that these items had probably belonged to Lady Rachael's father. Rachael had lovingly saved one of her own father's white shirts. She'd wear it when she needed to feel close to him.

"Nathaniel's life is on the line—no time for memories," she reminded herself as she yanked on the trousers, buttoned up the shirt and pulled her hair back. She had no time to fight with a corset. In the dark, she hoped that she would look like a young boy. She had to protect Nathaniel, but first, she had to find him.

"Was this how it all came down the last time, Lady Rachael?" she murmured, pinning her hair up under the cap. "Am I just repeating your mistakes?" She knew that her favorite ghost would choose not to answer. She had to be smart, figure this out on her own, and rely on her instincts.

"Mazie?" she whispered through the crack in the door, shining the candle inside, "Mazie, wake up." Nathaniel had moved Mazie to an adjoining room that must have served as a nursery at one time. Rachael didn't protest, Mazie being near gave her a bit of comfort.

"Mazie?" she whispered again louder, hearing a slight snore in the darkness.

"M'lady, what … what is it? Is that you? Are you sick?"

"Shhh," Rachael hushed her.

"M'lady, why are you dressed like that?" Mazie sat up, rubbing her eyes.

"There's someone outside. I think we are in danger. I'm going to try to make my way to the Captain's house," Rachael whispered.

"You can't go out there alone, m'lady. I'll go with you." She jumped out of her bed, pulling on a set of man's pants that she dragged out from under her bed.

"Mazie?" Rachael pointed to the pants.

"Left over from a few years ago," she giggled.

"Shhh," she warned her again and blew out the candle. "Come."

They made their way down the back stairs in the pitch black. As she hurried, Rachael slipped off one of the stairs and almost fell, but caught herself as her ankle twisted. She muffled a cry as a sharp pain shot down her foot and up her leg. Mazie stopped, but Rachael signaled her to keep going.

Cracking the back door a bit, Rachael stood like a statue, listening. There wasn't a sound outside. Waving

Mazie forward, they made their way to a thorny bush next to the barn. She guessed that the path besides the building would lead to Main Street and Nathaniel's house. She couldn't ask Mazie so she had to trust her instincts that this was the way. Mazie pointed to the path and began to speak, but Rachael shushed her again and signaled for her to follow closely behind her.

The stones jabbed Rachael's feet through the silk slippers. Her ankle ached as well, but she continued to pick her way along the path. Branches whipped across her face and arms as she scurried down a steep little hill. A sliver of moon cast little light on the opening.

Turning a dark corner, Rachael felt herself lifted up off the ground by a strong arm around her waist. A large hand clamped across her mouth so she could neither breathe nor scream. Had she fallen into a trap by leaving the house? They had her. Nathaniel would never find her or know what happened to her. She kicked, elbowed him in the chest, and then, the smell of spice enveloped her.

"Ouch. Stop squirming. It's me, Nathaniel," he pressed his lips against her ear and turned her around in one powerful move so she faced him. Rachael threw her arms around his neck and whispered, "I'm so happy to see you."

"Are you alright?" His breath in her ear sent tingles through her.

"I am. But how did you know? Why are you here?" she murmured, nuzzling against his neck. She almost blurted out about Lady Rachael's warning, but at the last second, thought better of it. He would think her ridiculous.

He gave her a quick kiss. "I knew that Philip and Edwin would move against you quickly, tonight. Shhh."

Someone pushed through the brush. "M'lady, where are you?" a little voice whispered.

Nathaniel grasped Mazie's hand and yanked her towards them as he slid Rachael slowly down his body to the ground. The man did have a way about him.

"Shhh," Nathaniel warned again. He shuffled Mazie and Rachael behind him at the sound of approaching feet.

Rachael ran her hand along his back. He wore no jacket, but his shirt was soft and silky. She put her other hand on his waist, trying to peek around him. He caressed her fingers softly. She looked up at him and squeezed his hand, sensing her loss already.

Two men appeared out of the bush.

Rachael felt Nathaniel's muscles stiffened under her touch and then relax.

"Captain, what do you want us to do with the men we caught?" They stood shrouded in the darkness facing Nathaniel.

"Tie them up and throw them in the barn while I bring Rachael back to the house. Was Master Philip among them?"

"We caught him climbing the trellis to her Lady's room. Two others were hiding behind the barn. Master Philip had a pistol in his hand. Sir Edwin was nowhere to be found."

"I'll be right there. Don't let them out of your sight." Nathaniel's tone said it all.

"Yes, Captain." The men turned and melted into the blackness.

Turning to Rachael, Nathaniel stated, "How careless of me, leaving you alone in that house. You could have been taken tonight or worse, shot dead by your brother. How did you know you were in danger? You should have been asleep."

She hesitated, thinking of a way to answer him without mentioning Lady Rachael's warning. "I couldn't sleep...."

"I don't mean to interrupt, m'lady, but I should return to the house to cook breakfast for the Captain's men. I see the morning sky starting to break."

Mazie provided Rachael time to come up with a legitimate answer to Nathaniel's question.

"By all means, Mazie, and thank you for coming with me tonight."

"Oh m'lady, no, thank you for including me in this adventure. I'll always be by your side." Mazie gave a little bow, turned and ran back into the shadows.

Rachael faced the east and there, a beautiful new day stretched its pink, gold and purple fingers across the horizon. A smile spread across her face—she was so thankful to be here, in this century, with this man, for at least another day.

"Why were you out here on the path?" Nathaniel pulled Rachael against his chest, wrapping her safely in his arms. "And why are you wearing that big smile when you were almost kidnapped or worse?"

"How can you not smile when another sunrise finds us together?" She touched his face. "As I was saying, I couldn't sleep and was sitting at the desk reading… writing in my diary when I heard something outside. I decided that if it were Philip and his men, I couldn't fight them alone, I needed you. I woke Mazie and we ran out here in the dark. I only worried that I'd lose my way." The words slipped out. Damn, her mother was correct again—too truthful.

"Why would you think that? You have taken this path to town many times?" He held her back, delving into her eyes. "You scratched your face."

"One of the vines as I ran. It's nothing."

"Are you sure?" he touched her cheek.

She covered his hand, "Yes. I've not taken the path in the dark and not under stress like tonight." Did he suspect? "I was frightened." She had to be careful not to show that she didn't know where the path led.

"Until I find Edwin, I don't want you to be alone. Your brother was Edwin's pawn. Now that Philip's out of the picture, Edwin will think up another way to get what he wants—you."

"He won't succeed." She put on a positive face for him as they walked the path back up to the house, his hand massaging her neck. But in truth, she had no idea what Edwin brought to this battle.

"Do you think he will try again—soon?" she asked as they reach the kitchen door.

"Are you hurt? You seem unsteady, my love."

"I slipped down those dar-"—she hesitated—"dark stairs. I'm fine."

"Should I carry you upstairs?"

She laughed, knowing that he would love to do that. "No, of course not. But tell me what you think Edwin will do now that Philip has been stopped."

"I don't mean to frighten you, but he'll come after you again. You have to be on your guard—always. He desires you and your inheritance. Edwin struck a bargain with Philip for you and, in return, he'll grant your brother Rose Hill."

"Never will he have Rose Hill—never. And you already have me." She tried to lighten the mood, make him smile. "So he wastes his time and effort."

"We will marry as soon as you are ready. I don't know what I would do if I lost you. You mesmerize me so that I can think of nothing else but you since my return." He scanned her outfit—a titled cap, a pair of her father's pants and one of his long blue tailored shirts.

"Where did these clothes come from Rachael?" He lifted off the hat and reached for her hair pins.

"Do I no longer bewitch you dressed in my father's clothes?" Rachael joked. "Should I seek another?"

His face clouded over. "I would be most unhappy with that. You are more my love now than ever. As I said, you are very different."

"How?" she pressed again, wanting to know as much as she could about the woman that she inhabited.

"I mean you no disrespect, my beauty, but two years ago you never would have dressed in clothes like these with your hair tied up. And certainly would never have allowed me see you like this. You would have fainted at the sight of those men and at Edwin's tirade; and you would have run crying into my arms. Your father's illness and death have accomplished much. Instead, you have grown fearless, sometimes to a fault. You'll not be intimidated by any man, including me."

She interrupted him, "Isn't that good? And you never intimidate me. You are a strong, caring, protective man."

"I'm not always that way as you'll see when I deal with your brother and Edwin. You are everything to me Rachael—you always will be. I wish to spend my entire life and more with you."

His words touched her so. "And I with you, my Captain." She stood on tip toe and kissed him. She would be his forever. Lady Rachael would not have him back. Rachael knew now that this man belonged with her. She wouldn't leave him, no matter what.

A clearing of the throat interrupted them. "Captain, shall I leave the captives tied in the barn for now?" The man looked only at Nathaniel and not at Rachael so as to not embarrass her.

Nathaniel draped his arm possessively around Rachael's shoulder. "I'll be right out, Dennis. Mazie is preparing breakfast for us—please call the men in. I have an announcement to make." He stared down at Rachael with a smoldering look that made her legs weak.

"Yes Captain." His man grinned and left as quickly and quietly as he had entered.

"I will run upstairs and change. I hate these awful slippers." She yanked them off, threw them on the stairs and stood barefoot in front of him.

His look traveled down to her bare feet and slowly back up to her eyes. "You love those silly things. What's going on with you?" He reached to unbutton the top button on her shirt.

"My Captain, how forward of you." She clasped his hand as it moved to the next one. His hand brushed against her skin, igniting a new fire in her.

"I want to see if you still wear my opal." His grin betrayed his words.

"Really?" Rachael reached in and pulled out the opal on the chain. "I'm never without it. Know that it nestles nicely." She extended it to him as his eyes delved deeply into hers.

"You are sassy and very forward, my love." He whispered in her ear, moving his hand across her neck. "And before you make me carry you up those stairs, I'll go and speak to your brother while you change." He tugged on her shirt and dropped the opal inside, his hand lingering against her breast before he kissed her, turned, and left the kitchen.

Chapter Fourteen

Rachael strode past the looking glass that lay face down on the vanity. That's what her mother had called hand mirrors—looking glasses. She had told her that they possessed magical powers and could turn things upside down and backwards. And Lady Rachael's looking glass had proven her correct. It played the innocent one laying there with its gold scrolls and lovely violets, but Rachael knew better. It had exercised its magic, transported her here and could propel her back to the twenty-first century, of that she had no doubt.

As furious as Lady Rachael must be watching the bond between Rachael and Nathaniel grow, she could do nothing if Rachael ignored the hand mirror. And furthermore, Rachael knew that Lady Rachael had more work for her to do.

Standing in front of the floor mirror, Rachael adjusted her dress until it flowed perfectly. She moved to the desk where the journal lay open. She read:

It's not over, Rachael. Protect Nathaniel—I know you can do it. I couldn't. Look to those closest to him. Be alert. Edwin will not give up.

The room swayed and Rachael's knees buckled. She knew it—there was more to come. Rachael scribbled:

Who is it, Rachael? You have to tell me more. How can I help Nathaniel when I don't know who or what to expect?

She waited… nothing appeared.

"Really? You expect me to save Nathaniel with those few words of wisdom?" Exasperated, she whacked the diary and watched it fly off the table. It struck the wooden floor with a loud clunk.

"He'll die because I won't be able to save him and you'll blame me this time. Help me, for God's sake!" Her frustration rose.

Even knowing how Rachael felt about Nathaniel, Lady Rachael urged her to save him. Or would it be she who saved him? Rachael picked up the diary, placed it on the desk and flipped the pages, looking again for some written guidance. Nothing.

"God damn it all to hell, Rachael. What do you want me to do?"

"M'lady? Are you alright?" Mazie asked, standing in the doorway. "The Captain asked me to check on you. We heard noises and talking up here and he... we were worried. You are so pale."

How long had Mazie had been standing there and what had she heard? "Mazie...," Rachael started to explain.

"M'lady, please. I'm your maid and whatever we say or do stays between us. Now what can I do for you?"

Mazie and Carolyn had stayed with her till the end because they could be trusted.

"Thank you Mazie. Only a drink of water, please. I need to break my fast." Her voice sounded weak. "It's been a long night and neither of us slept much." Rachael hadn't slept at all and was exhausted, but knew she couldn't let her guard down.

She scanned the blank pages. Lady Rachael's words had all disappeared. She slammed the book close, sipping the water that Mazie had handed her while Mazie busied herself cleaning the vanity, picking up the mirror and placing it back after she dusted.

"I'm better, Mazie, thank you." She bypassed the vanity where the looking glass lay facing the ceiling. It wasn't time.

"Let's go down and join the others."

Rachael still had work to do, but only Lady Rachael knew what it entailed and she wasn't telling.

Chapter Fifteen

All talk ceased as Rachael entered the dining room. The men jumped up. Nathaniel rushed to her side.

"How pale you are, Rachael. Maybe you should have stayed upstairs and rested, my love?" His concern for her was written all over his face. He loved his Rachael so. "I sent Mazie up to check. I thought I heard noises and voices and feared for you," he whispered in her ear as he pulled her chair out.

"I'm fine, really. I'm such a klutz. I knocked my diary off the desk and was berating myself for being so stupid." Rachael's eyes went to Mazie who continued laying out the silverware without looking up at her. Whatever she had heard, she would say nothing.

"A what?" Nathaniel whispered in her ear. "Careful, Rachael."

She turned to see the quizzical look in his eyes. Did he suspect something when she had slipped up in her language? He was correct; she would have to be more careful.

"I'm just so careless sometimes." She looked directly at Nathaniel as he watched her. "I'm in need of some food as you all must be as well. It has been a long night. Please sit all." Nathaniel pushed in her chair as she sat at the head of the table, his hand resting on her shoulder.

"Mazie, please bring in the meal for these good men. They must be famished."

"Yes, m'lady. Can I bring something for you?" Her concern showed in her eyes. "I'll bring your regular breakfast, but would you like coffee or tea?"

Rachael smiled at Mazie. "Yes, Mazie, coffee please. I'm fine, really. Please have Carolyn start serving."

Mazie gave a little bow and disappeared into the kitchen.

"You know most of my crew, Rachael. Arnold and Franklin are the newest." Nathaniel stated.

"Look to those closest to him" echoed in Rachael's head, the latest piece of the puzzle from Lady Rachael.

She scanned the two new crewmembers' faces wondering which one could be the threat to Nathaniel. She would find out and expose him.

Nathaniel surprised her by raising her hand in his. "I want you all to know that Rachael has agreed to be my wife. She wears my betrothal ring." A cheer went up. "Most of you were with me as I searched the world for the stones that befit my beautiful bride. As you can see, the search was well worth it." He kissed Rachael's hand and whispered, "I love you."

She felt her face flush as she looked up into his gold flecked grey eyes. She clasped his hand with both of hers and mouthed, "I love you too."

"Captain, we are very happy for you and for Rachael. M'lady, he is a good man, our Captain is," his first mate, Dennis, announced.

Rachael focused on Nathaniel, but spoke to his men. "I know better than any of you what a good man he is and I will protect him from all harm as he shields me."

"Look to those closest to him."

Smiling, she searched the eyes of each of them, watching for one to look away. Arnold held her stare, but Franklin turned away and toyed with his food. It had to be him. Lady Rachael was warning her to be careful of him. Her heart rate accelerated.

"There is nothing I wouldn't do to save him from harm." Her smile belied the consequences of the promise that she had just made to them, especially as she observed Franklin.

"She is the woman I have waited for all my life. We will be married here at Rose Hill before we sail next."

A cheer went up with clapping and yelling. Franklin looked up from his plate at Nathaniel and to her. Rachael stared him down, sending him a mental message,

You will be very sorry if you harm him. I will hunt you down like a dog. That's my promise to you.

Chapter Sixteen

Rachael bundled up on the swing, an afghan flung across her lap, Nathaniel's arm around her shoulders. Resting her head on his chest, she listened to the strong and constant rhythm of his heart. He couldn't have died almost two hundred years ago. She couldn't wrap her mind around this parallel universe, this dream that she was in.

"What are you thinking, Rachael? You have been very quiet since dinner." Nathaniel drew the slipping afghan up around her.

She shook her head. "Things you would never understand, things that even I don't understand."

"Try me; I may surprise you, my love. Do you think I wouldn't appreciate any troubles you might have? What kind of marriage is this to be…?"

"I wish you could …. But they are not the kind of problems that you can resolve. I think these are mine to solve alone."

"With me by your side, you'll never again have to do anything by yourself. You never know how I might be of help. When we are called on to take a stand, we often rise to the occasion. You're capable of doing whatever it is that you have to do. I have to do what I'm called on to carry out as well." His cryptic reply sounded as though he knew what she faced and that he would confront it as well. His voice had a curious, almost sad tone to it. Could he know what was about to happen?

"I question my strength to do it. And not knowing exactly what it is I'm heading into makes it all the more complicated."

"I don't understand why you doubt yourself. You're strong and intelligent. When the time comes, we'll do what we have to do Rachael, no matter what." As he spoke, his gaze went somewhere beyond the veranda into the garden.

She analyzed his face. He had a strong profile with sharp features, chiseled as she described them in her novels, with a square jaw. Without his beard, the clef in his chin was visible making him even more handsome tonight, if that were possible.

"Are you committing me to memory, my love, so that when I'm gone, you can close your eyes and remember me as I am this night?" He continued to look out at the darkness.

He read her mind. "I guess I am. You take my breath away sometimes. Is that wrong—I mean, to sear you into my consciousness?"

"You plan for the future, for the worse. Very unlike my Rachael." He turned holding her stare. "We have much to share about ourselves, but those things can wait until you are safe, until this is done."

"You are in danger too."

"I'm always in danger—that's my life," he joked.

"This is different. I fear Edwin will try to kill you, not me. I think he has infiltrated your crew." Her eyes stung thinking that she might not be able to protect him, that he might be killed in this house again, or worse, on his ship when she wasn't near. How did Lady Rachael move past his death? Maybe she didn't, which was why Rachael was here…?

"How do you know this?" He broke into her thoughts.

"I can't explain, but I think it might be Franklin, one of your new men." The moon moved slightly overhead, casting a soft light on the sun dial as though highlighting that their hours were numbered. "When did he show up?"

"I hired him a day ago on the wharf. He appeared looking for a position on the ship. I suspected something wasn't right about him."

"So why did you hire him?"

"Better to know your enemy and have him close, correct?" A few seconds passed as he glanced over the garden area once again. "I was thinking—would you like to marry on the twentieth? A beautiful Sunday in the spring with a full moon?" His eyes never stopped scrutinizing the shadows.

"How can you even think of a wedding when you know your life's in danger? When one or both of us may not live past tonight?" Frustration crept into her voice.

"My love, do you not think I can protect myself as well as you? How can you choose such a weak man for your husband?" he teased. "Life will continue, I promise. You need to design your wedding dress and make arrangements for the day." He leaned in and kissed her. "Let's move inside. There's a chill in the air." His eyes moved once again to the murkiness cast by the slight moon overhead.

Chapter Seventeen

April 8th 1804

"Ouch!" A pin pierced Rachael's side. She held her breath as she stood on the small stepstool in her bedroom and the seamstress worked on fitting her wedding dress. Four days ago, when she entered this house for an estate sale, she never could have imagined that she would be standing here being fitted for a wedding dress for her marriage to a sea captain. If only she could share with Kayla how this incredible man had opened up her heart again. He made her feel alive. She laughed. She might feel alive, but he had been dead two hundred years. Rachael knew that Kayla would love him too if she could get by the ghost stuff.

"I'm so sorry, m'lady," Esther remarked in a soft voice. She had appeared in the late afternoon carrying a small black satchel containing all of her sewing apparatus. She knelt with pins in her mouth, plucking them quickly and placing them where needed. The frown on her face coupled with the pulled back mousey brown hair made her appear older than her twenty-five years. Her fingers flew as she laid Nathaniel's gorgeous Irish lace over the silk low cut bodice and draped it to form a long train that started at the deep V-shape at the back of Rachael's waist. The gown would be the exact one in the portrait that Rachael had first glimpsed when she entered Rose Hill.

"It's fine, Esther. Are we almost finished?" Rachael shifted a bit. She had been standing in this position for two hours. First, there was a very cute muslin dress, followed by the wedding night nightgown with a cover, then an embroidered satin gown, and now the wedding dress.

"Captain Nathaniel is here to see you, m'lady. Shall I ask him to wait?" Mazie interrupted.

"Of course, Mazie. Tell him I'll be down in a few minutes. Thank you. And please make him some tea?"

"Esther, can we finish this tomorrow?" How could she thank Nathaniel for saving her from this torture? She could think of a few ways, but they wouldn't be acceptable for a young lady to voice in this century. She laughed, thinking how scandalous she would be perceived.

"Yes, m'lady?"

"Nothing Esther, I was just thinking about something the Captain had said," she fibbed.

"You and the Captain are so perfect for each other. I can see your love for him in your eyes and his love reflected back. It will be such a happy day when you marry."

"Thank you, Esther. It can't come soon enough. The wedding gown looks exquisite."

"M'lady, the beauty comes from you, not the material. I think I have enough to work on with all these dresses. I'll bring them back in a few days for you to try on." She gathered all the pieces and parts and handed them to her apprentice. She bowed and left the room.

Rachael sat down at the desk to rest her feet, enjoying a few moments of quiet. The journal was open. Words began to appear.

The time is near Rachael. Protect yourself and Nathaniel. I love the man dearly. You will soon know the rest. I know you can save him.

Lady Rachael wrote in riddles. Rachael wrote on the page…

What is the rest?
How can I protect him? Please help me...

She waited. Nothing more appeared.

What did she mean by 'the rest?' Did she realize that Rachael's nineteenth century life had become too precious to her to abandon it? Did she know that Rachael didn't want to give Nathaniel back to her?

"I don't understand what the rest is?" she pleaded out loud.

Her fingers fumbled as she fastened the hooks on the back of a black and white ribbon muslin dress with hand painted flowers covering the skirt. The bodice fell off her shoulders with short loose fluffy cap sleeves. It was stunning on her, on Lady Rachael.

She pictured Nathaniel pacing in the sitting room, waiting for her. She would leave his world soon enough, sadly, but for now, she would enjoy every moment with him. She checked the journal once more—the page remained empty.

"Lady Rachael, you are no help at all. How can I protect him if you don't share what you know?"

Putting on her white slippers, Rachael started down the stairs to the sitting room. Halfway down, she heard voices—a man and a woman. It was not Nathaniel. The male voice was one that she didn't recognize. The woman's voice—was it Carolyn's? Did she have a boyfriend who came to visit her? A form moved by the bottom of the stairs. Rachael melted back into the darkness hoping it would shield her. The man, Franklin, gave a quick look up the stairs and moved on. She was sure her breathing could be heard throughout the entire house. After waiting a few minutes, she ran down the rest of the stairs hiking her skirts high in a very unladylike manner. She dashed along the hallway to the sitting room. No Nathaniel. She froze. Was she too late? Had they already kidnapped him?

"Rachael, is that you?" a male voice came from the formal parlor across the hall.

She glided across the hallway in her new soft shoes right into his open arms.

"That was quite an entrance. You look beautiful."

His smile intoxicated her. She reached up and circled her arms around his neck, so glad that he was safe. "I was afraid... I was too late."

He cocked his eyebrow. "Too late for what, my love? I will not leave without you ever." Again he spoke in riddles.

"Some things are out of our control. Could you check that all my hooks are fastened on the back of my dress? I tried to reach all of them, but I guess I need longer arms."

"Or you could have engaged Mazie?"

"She was busy with dinner and I'd rather have you do it, if you don't mind." Was she being too forward?

"Your wish is my command, my love. This is the first time you have entrusted me with such a personal task." He watched for her reaction.

She gave him a smile. "Is it something that you have no experience doing? Maybe you are better at unhooking them?"

He spun her around and she felt his hand move up her back as he pushed her hair to the side and touched the top hook.

"Did you say to unhook them?" His hand played along the back of her neck. "You play a very dangerous game with me, little one."

"Do I? I don't mean to." She did and he knew it. She struggled to regain her composure as he brought her closer.

"Whether you mean to or not, you tempt me far too much these days." When she turned to face him, he kissed her and whispered in her ear, "I will love you forever, my

Rachael, never forget that. No matter what happens, I will search the entire world for you." His eyes reflected sadness for a moment.

"What's going to happen, Nathaniel, tell me?"

"I don't know. I wish I could tell you, but whatever happens, just remember that I will find you, my love. That's my promise to you."

He emphasized the word 'you' or was her mind running wild? "You think I'm to be taken—by Edwin?" Now he frightened her because Edwin would torture Lady Rachael or maybe even kill her. He would force himself on her. Rachael couldn't bear him pawing and drooling all over her. She didn't want to be in Nathaniel's world without him. That's why she avoided the mirror. He should know how she felt, how Lady Rachael felt.

"If Edwin takes you, Nathaniel, or worse, I will leave immediately. I won't stay here without you." She couldn't say it any plainer.

"Nor I without you. Don't worry my sweet, after tonight we will live a long life together." He pushed her hair over her bare shoulder, touching the opal that snuggled between her breasts. The touch of his hand on her breast sent electric jolts through her.

"Tonight?" She wrapped her arms around him wanting this moment to last forever. But she knew better. The time must be near.

He pointed to the fireplace with his right hand, holding her close with his left. "Don't you think that would be a perfect place for our wedding portrait, on the wall above the fireplace? Someday, when we are old and grey, we will sit here on this very couch and remember that beautiful April day...."

Another ripple ran through her. The wall was empty. She looked at him and saw something in his eyes, a flicker of knowledge?

"It's a perfect place." Her voice softened as she thought of the portrait of Lady Rachael alone that hung there just four days ago in another world far away. She remembered Lady Rachael's loss, his death.

"Rachael, what's wrong? You're ashen." He took her elbow and sat with her on the sofa facing the fireplace.

"I was just thinking of the future…." She took his hand. "I think it's close, like you do. Whatever they are going to do, it will be soon, tonight maybe? I heard voices as I came down the stairs, saw shadows running…."

He looked away. "I agree. That's why we're here Rachael, you and I. We'll work through this danger tonight as a team and we'll make it, I promise you. We will be together, somehow, at some point; we'll be together."

He relaxed her with his curious answer.

"That's a good thing for a couple soon to be married, don't you think, to be able to work well as a team —to survive? To be married and live happily ever after?"

"Your color and sassiness are returning. On another subject, how did the fittings go today? Torturous?"

He thought it funny that she was poked with pins.

"That's not the appropriate response to give your wife-to-be when she stood in one place for hours, pins piercing her magnificent body, reams of material draped over her, discussions of every part of her body by everyone present."

He raised an eyebrow, "A discussion I would have loved to have joined in on."

Before she had a chance to respond, the sound of glass breaking filled the room. Nathaniel grabbed her hand. "Act naturally. You and I can make it through this. You know we can. Give me a kiss for good luck."

She kissed him, not knowing what they would face in the next few minutes. His lips lingered.

"I love you," he whispered. "Let's go. It's time."

Chapter Eighteen

Nathaniel and Rachael strode through the dining room door, hand in hand. Mazie stood by the table, with her hands on her hips, shaking her head.

"Are you alright, Mazie? It's fine, don't worry, there are more glasses." Rachael consoled her, almost relieved that it was simply an accident.

"Oh no, m'lady, it wasn't me. I heard it break and when I arrived, there was no one here and the glass lay smashed on the floor. Puzzling...."

Lady Rachael's writings rang true. It would happen tonight. They were waiting for them somewhere in the house. Nathaniel sensed it too, she could tell by the look on his face.

He squeezed her hand and whispered, "It ends tonight. Know I love you forever, my Rachael. Remember that, no matter what happens. Be strong." He kissed her ear lobe.

"Nathaniel, I love you as well. Please take care... for me. We have our wedding ...."

He kissed her hand, turned and backed out of the room, his finger to his lips.

Her heart hurt as she thought that this might be the last time she would see him alive. She couldn't think that way. Her job was to keep him alive—somehow.

Mazie stared at them both, not knowing what was happening.

"All is well, Mazie. Let's sweep up this mess and set the table for dinner." Rachael winked at her, trying to convey that everything would be alright.

"Yes, m'lady. Carolyn is finishing up dinner in the kitchen now. I'll go find the broom," Mazie responded leaving the room.

Carolyn had been the female voice that Rachael had heard from the stairs. Franklin must have befriended her so he could gain access to the house. Shadows outside played off the French doors. The drapes swayed but there was no wind.

Rachael wiped damp palms on her skirt and felt a lump inside the pocket. It felt like a small pistol? She traced it with her fingers. The gun hadn't been there when she put on the dress.

"Thank you, Lady Rachael," she whispered. Had she used it the first time that Nathaniel was shot? She only had to make sure that she didn't shoot Mazie, Nathaniel or herself by mistake. She could shoot a gun, but a nineteenth century version? Could she handle it?

As she removed another glass from the chest and placed it on the table, she heard voices and a thumping in the hallway.

"Rachael, run!" Nathaniel's voice rang out. She started for the French doors when she realized that she couldn't leave him alone to fight this battle. That's why she had been transported here, to help him. She fingered the gun. If it ended here, it would end here for both of them. She wouldn't let Lady Rachael live in this house by herself again, mourning him for all her long lonely life. The last page of her journal would be erased. There would be no wedding portrait and no Haverford descendants unless Rachael saved Nathaniel.

A pistol shot ran out.

Mazie flew through the door, terror in her eyes and her hand to her mouth. "Oh m'lady…m'lady…the Captain has been shot."

"Oh God, No..." Rachael wailed, pushing Mazie aside, taking the pistol from her pocket. "No.... Nathaniel.... nooooooooo."

Chapter Nineteen

Nathaniel stood in the corridor, fighting off three men. Carolyn remained frozen by the back door, covering her mouth with her hands, horror in her eyes. "I'm sorry, m'lady, I didn't know he would do such a thing...."

Rachael turned to Nathaniel struggling with one of the men. "Leave him alone." Her voice rang strong. The three men turned, looked at each other, and laughed. They actually mocked her, the fools.

"Run, Rachael, run... please." Nathaniel pleaded, with such love and sorrow in his eyes. "I'm sorry...."

"They are laughing at me, Nathaniel. Run my a...," She caught herself. "I told you to leave him alone, but you laugh at me instead?"

She raised the gun. Her first shot hit the one who laughed the loudest. He yelped, falling to the floor grabbing his leg. Her second shot hit the one at Nathaniel's throat. He screamed and grabbed at his shoulder. The third man, Franklin, backed away, the smile wiped off his face.

"Is it funny now? Run, I beg you—turn and run." Her voice echoed down the hall, through the house. "If you aren't going to run, then get your ass down on the floor."

He started to turn, but stopped as she smiled coldly at him. "Go ahead. I've already shot the leg and the shoulder—for you, Franklin, if that's your real name, it will be the head or the heart. Run, I said. Make my day." Rachael watched Nathaniel struggle to stand against the wall, blood oozing out from under his cuff onto the floor.

Rachael's fury built as she walked up to Franklin. "Did you hear me? I said run, you bastard, run!" She struck him so hard across the face with the butt of the pistol that she thought she heard his jaw crack. "You turncoat bastard."

Suddenly, three men rushed through the door and tackled him. It was Nathaniel's crew, led by Dennis.

"M'lady, are you hurt?" Dennis asked.

"No, I'm fine, but the Captain's been shot, please help him," she pleaded, running to Nathaniel as he slid down the wall, losing consciousness.

Chapter Twenty

"Stop fussing, Rachael. I'm fine." Nathaniel leaned back on her bed. Dennis yanked off his boots. Nathaniel winced as he moved his shoulder but said nothing.

"You have lost a lot of blood, but it's a clean shot right through the flesh and should heal well. I doused the wound with alcohol to cleanse it and the bleeding has stopped. You need to rest now." She was rambling, she knew. A nervous habit of hers and hopefully, one of Lady Rachael's as well.

"I'll leave you to tend to him, m'lady. I wish you well. He's usually not a very good patient."

She smiled. "Why does that not surprise me, Dennis? Thank you for everything you and the crew did. I can handle him from here, I think." She winked at him.

"I truly think you can, m'lady. You were unusually brave tonight standing up to those thugs. In doing so, you saved our Captain's life. He has chosen well with you. You are indeed his match." He turned to Nathaniel. "Captain, I'll check in tomorrow to see what you and your lady might need."

"Dennis, my heartfelt thanks to you and the crew for saving the day. Rachael will see to my needs."

"It was your lady who saved the day, Captain. She's quite a shot. If I were you, I would obey her orders," Dennis joked, backed away and shut the door behind him.

Nathaniel struggled to sit up as Rachael plumped the pillows behind him.

"Why didn't you run when I called out to you? You could have been killed." He leaned back against the pillows, his face gray and sweaty. "Dennis is correct, you are quite a shot. I'll have to be careful. When did you learn to shoot like that?" He grabbed her hand and brought it to his lips before she could move away.

"I couldn't leave you to fight alone if there was to be a wedding portrait, now could I? What kind of a wife-to-be would I be? And what would people say if it was just me standing there in the painting—poor Rachael, her Captain was shot and killed in the hallway as she ran away?" Rachael had seen how pathetic Lady Rachael looked hanging there alone and how her writings in her journal expressed what it felt like to live in this house after her love was murdered.

"I knew we could make it together. And Father taught me to shoot many years ago. He always said a woman could never be too careful." That was not a lie; Rachael's own father had taught her to how to handle a gun.

"Tiny, isn't it?" She took the pistol from her pocket and turned it over in her hand. She still questioned how it ended up there. It had to be Lady Rachael at work. "Now you know that I can protect us both."

He laughed and then winced from the pain.

"You'd better not laugh at me. You saw what happened to the men who did." Now it was her turn to joke with him. "You should rest. Do we know where Edwin is? I didn't see him here tonight." She ignored the blood stains on her skirt and rubbed the pistol on the clean portion, still fearing this episode wasn't over.

"Are you going to shoot him too?" He made fun of her.

"If I have to kill him to keep you alive, yes, I will." Her tone was serious.

He watched her with an inquisitive look on his face. "Well, maybe he was lucky that I dealt with him and not you. As we speak, Edwin is sailing to Liverpool, England where he'll live out the rest of his miserable days locked away. He's wanted for murdering a wealthy woman in

England, a woman who was his wife. He forced her to marry him, like he tried to do with you, and when her children attempted to have the marriage annulled and the will changed, he killed her so he could inherit her money. He hid out here using her title." He took the pistol from her, laid it on the bed, and took her hands in his good one. "He would have killed you too eventually to take over your family's fortune."

"I knew that. But now, we're all okay, true? Edwin's gone, Philip's no longer a threat—you and I are safe?"

He kissed her hands. "I love you, Rachael. Yes, we're safe." His eyes held sadness.

Her heart felt a squeeze. She knew that her time with him was coming to an end.

"Why aren't you happy? We're alive and life will continue on—we'll wed on a gorgeous Sunday, April twentieth. You'll give me children to watch over me..." Her voice cracked as she tried to convince him of all the happiness that lay ahead for them when she knew that her life was about to shatter into pieces, like the mirror.

"If all is good, why then are you crying?"

"Tears of happiness... isn't that what women do? Cry when they are happy and when they're sad."

She caressed his face, tracing every detail with her fingers. She would never forget the grey eyes that flashed with a touch of gold, his long strong nose and soft pliable lips, a dimple on one side when he smiled, and a deep clef in his chin. When she returned to the twenty-first century, she would live the rest of her life in love with a sea captain who lived over two hundred years ago. And she wouldn't even have a grave to visit because he would probably be buried at sea thousands of miles away. Sorrow pierced her soul. The tears spilled over onto her cheeks.

"Make love to me Rachael, please. Here and now." His voice was hoarse. He swiped the tears from her cheeks.

"Please don't cry. Stay with me. Don't leave me, not now... not ever." He patted a spot next to him on the bed.

"I can't, Nathaniel, I would if I could, but I can't. You need to rest." She said the truth. She wanted to tell him why, but who would believe her story. She couldn't have him make love to her and then return without him; she would never go back if he touched her, she knew that for sure.

"Tell me why," he begged.

Rachael turned and walked to the desk. The journal lay open.

"Because I love you too much and because I would have to stay with you for all eternity."

"Is that so wrong? Is that bad, Rachael?" There was pleading in his voice that broke her heart. "I'll stay with you forever as well. Why is that wrong? Tell me... We love each other."

She looked down and read Lady Rachael's writing.

My Nathaniel lives because of you. Thank you.

Rachael picked up the pen and wrote:

I'm jealous of a dead woman. How can that be? Nathaniel is an amazing man... I will miss him so very much. But you already know that. He has made it hard for me to return to my life and I know that I will never find anyone like him. I have fallen deeply in love with your Captain. I'm so very sorry, Rachael.

She watched as words appear:

I understand, but I promise that you will live a happy life when you return. You will have your own Nathaniel.

Rachael's sobs intensified. Never, she wanted to write, never would she find someone to love like this man.

"Rachael, please don't," he begged again, trying to swing his legs off the bed so he could go to her.

She turned to take one more look at him, to sear his image into her memory; he was already scorched into her heart.

"Stay, please stay there, Nathaniel. If you touch me…." Walking to the vanity, she picked up the mirror. Her eyes locked with his one long last time. She saw such sadness etched on his face.

"Rachael, please…please don't leave me like this."

She had to do it now or she never would. God help her—she wanted him. She could remain in his arms and in his life so easily. But he would be waiting for Lady Rachael, not her, under the arbor, and she would marry him and have his children.

"I love you Nathaniel, with all my heart and soul, forever," she whispered.

She picked up the looking glass and gazed into the smooth shiny surface through her tears. Blue eyes smiled back at her. Rachael grabbed the opal at her neck. She heard thunder, the room shook and then she heard a loud snap. The mirror cracked. Rachael heard Nathaniel scream her name….

"Rachael, no…please, don't…please don't leave me…."

Part II

Time—the corrector when our judgments err. ~ Lord Byron

Chapter Twenty-One

A week later… Wellfleet, Massachusetts

"I can't understand why you won't tell me what happened at Ghost Haven?" Kayla hadn't let up on her questioning of Rachael over the last week. She suspected something, but could never imagine the truth.

"I told you that I had a strange dream after being at the house, that's all. It felt real, but …." She turned away from Kayla as she sloshed the wine around in her glass. "Anyway, I chose to buy the gazing ball and the sundial that Sarah found boxed in the barn. She had no use for them so I took them." Rachael pointed to the garden in front of the deck. "Adds a bit of interest, don't you think? And she donated some of Rose Hill's flowers as well which I planted yesterday. I bought a desk and a mirror, but haven't picked them up yet. What more can I say? That's all there is to it."

This last week, Rachael had been anchored on the deck chair, facing the harbor for hours at a time. She sat, gazed, remembered and waited for … what? He was gone… her life with him was over. Dead, they were all dead. She had cried her eyes out, but it didn't change anything. They were still all gone. She thought maybe if she wrote their story, she could reconnect with Nathaniel, Mazie, Carolyn… pull herself out of this funk.

When she had eventually dragged herself inside to write, the words simply wouldn't come. Anything that she wrote was flat and unemotional. She couldn't find the words needed to express what she had felt as Lady Rachael. And besides, it hurt too much to pull those feelings out and write them down on paper.

The only time that she left the house had been to go grocery shopping, not that she felt like eating, but with Kayla stopping by, she needed beer and snacks. Yet when she wandered the aisles, her eyes searched for Nathaniel. He had died centuries ago, but somehow his words kept replaying in her head, "I will find you my love, that's my promise to you."

Rachael had returned to Rose Hill a few days ago and remained outside alone sitting on the stairs of the veranda. She couldn't go in and see all that she had lived, loved and lost, all tattered and dusty.

She had even called her mother, thinking that reaching out to someone who was family might help her through this period of loss. Her mother had gone through it with her Dad. But, the first time she called, her stepfather had answered. She hung up. The second time that she called, her mother picked up. Her first words reprimanded Rachael for hanging up on Ralph—she made it quite clear that she thought it was rude of her. Given the tone of the conversation, Rachael made up a story about not having called in a while and just wanting to make sure everything was okay. Then she lied and said that she had a call on her other line and had to go. That call convinced her all the more that she couldn't open up to anyone about what she was going through.

Kayla poured Rachael more wine and grabbed herself another beer. They sat without speaking as the pink, grey and purple fingers of sunset walked across the water.

"There's more to this dream hooey, I can tell. You've been in a mood all week. It's not like you… what happened in that damn haunted house? Something did, I know." Kayla leaned forward, "And the telephone message you left me, what was that? Some work you had to do for the infamous ghostly Rachael?"

Rachael fibbed badly. Her Rose Hill adventure would be shared with Kayla eventually, but not yet, it was still too raw.

"It seemed funny to tease you, given our conversation that morning." She looked down and laughed. "It was good wasn't it? I bet it had you freaking out for a few minutes."

Kayla pushed on, "I tried to call you back but your phone went right to voicemail. You're weird sometimes, you know. And speaking of weird things, don't you think it's creepy that all of a sudden the family discovers all this hidden stuff that in a minute changes the entire story of the shooting? Please. The grandkids-cubed are trying to clean up their ancestor's reputation so they can sell that mausoleum." Kayla guzzled from her beer bottle.

"I'm going to bid on the house."

Kayla's feet dropped from the deck railing with a bang as she bolted straight up coughing. "Hack... Oh my God, I almost choked to death."

"You okay?" Kay was always so dramatic.

"I'm perfectly lucid, but you? Are you daft? Why in the world would you want to live there? It's creepy, Rachael. What the hell's going on with you? Talk to me." Kayla remained standing as though demanding a rational answer.

Rachael didn't have one. "Look, wouldn't it make a great B&B? We've talked about buying a house and running a B&B together, so why not Rose Hill? Look at the intriguing stories we could play up in the PR to attract guests—murder, mystery and ghosts. And the location and view—perfect. It has a big kitchen, spacious parlors with fireplaces and many bedrooms. It would be perfect with a little fixing up. We'd be turning them away."

"Oh no, not me. With my luck, I'd be stuck in the transparent lady's room and she'd be madder than hell flying around moaning every night …. Nope, not me." She stared at Rachael. "Why are you doing this? It's so unlike you."

Kayla would freak out if Rachael told her the truth so she told her a half truth. "It's the history of the house and the people who lived there, the beautiful love story between Lady Rachael and her Captain. I've always loved that century, you know that from college. It's a perfect story for me, my great American novel." Rachael lightened the conversation a little. "If I lived there, I could envision what took place the night the Captain was attacked; maybe write a more authentic story—maybe a Pulitzer Prize winner? You think?"

"I know that's not it. You don't yearn for any prize. And you aren't writing...why? And why do you call the ghost 'Lady' Rachael?"

"And the reason you didn't tell me her name was Rachael? Sarah called her 'Lady Rachael' so she wouldn't confuse the two of us."

"I didn't say anything because I thought you'd be spooked. That's why I didn't want you to go there. But do you listen to me...oh, no. What do I know about ghosts, right?"

"Well, thanks for sparing me. And you think I wasn't spooked to hear it from weird Sarah in the haunted house, as you so kindly call it? And you know nothing about ghosts. Have you ever seen one, touched one... kissed one?"

"You're making my skin crawl, stop it."

"Wooooooooooo...it's getting dark. She'll be on the hunt soon or is it the haunt. We better go inside and hide."

After Kayla disappeared into the cottage, Rachael turned and whispered, "Goodnight my love, 'til we meet again."

Chapter Twenty-Two

As Rachael and Sarah sat on a swing on the crumbling veranda, Rachael asked, "I don't remember this swing being here before?" Was this a replica of the one she and Nathaniel had sat on when he proposed? Those memories washed over her bathing Rachael in his love once again.

She had returned to Rose Hill a number of times since her abrupt exit from the nineteenth century, but she hadn't had the courage to venture inside the house. Funny, she had the nerve to confront and shoot three long dead hooligans, but in this century, she didn't have the courage to step inside the house where she had lived and loved. Nathaniel would be so disappointed in her... and so would Vince.

"This? Have no idea; it simply appeared about a week ago. Nathaniel most likely. Hope the veranda supports our weight and this contraption," she laughed. Sarah's face, usually harsh and stern despite her youth, was transformed by the smile that she had inherited from Lady Rachael.

"It's such a tranquil spot isn't it? Feels like time stops...." Rachael could close her eyes and feel the warmth of Nathaniel's coat around her.

"I guess," Sarah remarked, tucking a curly strand of blond hair behind her ear. "Tell me again why you want to write this story about my family?" She interrupted Rachael's thoughts.

What could she say that she yearned to relive the love story between her great-great-great grandfather and herself by putting her feelings down on paper? That she, not the other Rachael, actually saved his life? That Sarah and her brother probably wouldn't even exist except for her? That she, Rachael, had lived Lady Rachael's life and loved Nathaniel more than her great-great-great grandmother ever could have?

"There's a number of unique stories revolving around your family's seafaring history that I'd like to capture—the background of this house for example, built by a man for his beautiful bride, or his striking young daughter who somehow ran a large shipping company in the 1800s, or a marriage between Rachael and her handsome sea captain. And then, there's always the mystery of the murder that was and then somehow never took place."

"You think people really care about that stuff? Well, you can waste your time figuring out who did what where—me, I don't really care. All in the past, and at this point has nothing to do with me. Do you have time to go inside?" Sarah asked, rising from the swing and causing it to sway. "You still interested in buying the house? Let's talk about it and then I'll have some ammunition for an adult discussion with my brother. Maybe you can talk some sense into him. His attachment to this house is bizarre."

Rachael coughed, trying to keep herself from laughing. Look who was calling who bizarre. She rose and followed Sarah to the door.

"In the meantime, you're welcome to use whatever material you come across that you can use for your story. I personally think you're wasting your time, but to each their own. The tale of my ancestors and this house are not as special as you think."

Oh, but they are—so very special, Rachael thought as she followed Sarah inside.

Rachael's eyes gradually adjusted to the darkness as she followed Sarah's shadowy form along the corridor. She could find her way through this house blindfolded. Her chest tightened, her head spun and her hands felt sweaty.

She leaned against the wall and took a deep breath… no, she wouldn't have a panic attack. She could do this.

She followed Sarah into the formal living room, the last place that Rachael and Nathaniel had discussed their wedding plans. She spotted a framed portrait sitting on a small side table. Nathaniel stood, handsome as ever, with his hand resting tenderly on Rachael's shoulder as she sat in front of him with a young tow-headed child playing at her feet.

Rachael's heart ached for the life they had lived together, for the child that they had created, for the love that they had shared. How pathetic—jealous of two people who had died hundreds of years ago.

Rachael felt Sarah watching her.

"I placed the portraits and photos around the room trying to create a little personal history of Rose Hill for anyone who might be interested in buying the property," Sarah stated with a disinterested tone. "No one has been beating down the door as you can see. I've been talking it up, but most people see only the costly restoration work needed to bring the house back to what it was. Have you thought any more about buying it?"

"Have you had any offers?"

"One, but it was just for the land and the bid was too low. He planned on knocking the house down and building condos if the town approved."

"I'm glad you turned it down…what a loss that would have been." Rachael fingered a daguerreotype photo, one where an older Rachael, hair streaked with gray pulled back at the nape of her neck and dressed in black, sat with a sad smile and her son standing behind her. She was a widow, Nathaniel was lost at sea, Rachael presumed. The young man was the image of his father, beard and all. Tears burned her eyes. Rachael had ended up alone at Rose Hill with his child to care for her, just as Nathaniel had foretold.

"I'm sorry," Rachael answered Sarah. "The photos say so much. It's hard to believe no one knew they were here until now. Where did you say they were found?" she asked, positioning the photograph back on the wobbly old mahogany side table.

"Nathaniel found them when he was cleaning out the tiny chamber off Lady Rachael's bedroom. He moved the old decrepit bed and a concealed panel in the wall popped open. Inside the cavernous space lay a box of old photos. The large covered wedding portrait leaned against the back wall." Sarah shook her head. "I can't even begin to imagine why they didn't rot over the centuries, but they looked perfect, like they were painted last week. And I guess no one knew the true story all these years… someone wanted to conceal it and wrote the fake diary to confuse the family." She turned to the fireplace. "And I have no idea who hung the portrait of Lady Rachael alone above the fireplace, but it only confirmed all the rumors. It must have been a pre-wedding portrait and for some reason, that's the one that hung here through the centuries. It supported all the false stories that she lived here alone after he was murdered."

All found in dear sweet Mazie's room. "It changes your entire perception of what their lives must have been, doesn't it? I gather fake accounts were passed down through the generations and no one thought to check them out? And to answer your initial question, yes, I have thought of buying Rose Hill. And I'd like to sit down with you and your brother at some point and discuss the price."

"When I hear from him, I'll pin him down for a date and time," Sarah responded, more animated than Rachael had ever seen her.

"That's fine. In the meantime, I have to figure out my finances. If I lived and wrote here, I'd be surrounded by your ancestor's history." Rachael rubbed her finger over the name engraved into the dusty leather-bound book that sat next to the photograph: "Haverford." She could hear Nathaniel's voice, "Mrs. Rachael Johnston Haverford, wife of Captain Nathaniel Rockford Haverford, a rather big name for such a tiny woman."

A jumble of events swirled around in Rachael's head. Had she really gone back and changed history? Had she dreamt it? Had those artifacts always existed in the forgotten space? Was she somehow tapping into the real truth? Whatever caused it, Sarah's family background had evolved into a happy tale of love, emotion and persistence— and Nathaniel's survival.

"Can you tell me what you know about their life?" Rachael's voice was hushed, reverent.

"I can't tell you much. Today's story is that when Lady Rachael's father died and Nathaniel returned from the sea, he was shot by someone for some reason. I still don't understand how he managed to live. It could be one of the same cast of characters who shot him in the first tale— Rachael herself, his crew or a jealous pursuer—and in the new story, they shot him again, but this time, he lived. Anyway, they married and he returned to sea. She remained here, pining away for him." She pointed to the painting above the fireplace. "That's the wedding portrait that my brother found. He hung the other portrait in the parlor."

The painting hung in the exact spot that Nathaniel had chosen two hundred years ago. Stepping back, Rachael stumbled over the frayed faded Oriental rug and landed in a cloud of dust on the faded maroon velvet sofa. She admired them—Nathaniel dressed in a long burgundy velvet formal jacket with a patterned gold and blue silk vest, his hand on the waist of the beautiful Rachael, she who wore a long cream silk empire waist dress accented with the off-white Irish lace.

How adorable Nathaniel had been the night that he carried the box filled with silk and lace into the parlor. If Rachael had accomplished anything, it was that Lady

Rachael would no longer stand alone in her portrait for eternity. Rachael had given Nathaniel back to her.

Large blue eyes smiled at Rachael as though thanking her. Did she detect a hint of sadness in Nathaniel's smoky eyes? She smiled... doubtful. He had his beautiful wife beside him. Oh, how she missed him. What a pitiful soul she was to be jealous of a couple who had been dead for over two hundred years, but she was envious.

Rachael coughed, suddenly aware of the billows of dust that rose around her. She waved at the dust, but the more she flapped, the more dust filled the air.

"Are you alright?" Sarah asked. "Come, move away from all that dirt."

"I'm... overwhelmed by the beauty of their wedding portrait." It wasn't a lie. "Here we all believed that he had been shot and killed in this house. I do remember the portrait of Lady Rachael that hung here. And Nathaniel found this new one?"

"As I said, in the tiny room off Lady Rachael's bedroom covered with an old piece of cloth behind trunks and boxes along with a diary and some old ratty men's clothes."

"They look so happy, don't they? Was there ever an arbor in the yard?" Rachael fired her questions rapidly. "You said that you found your great-great-great grandmother's journal, a different one from the one that was on her desk?" She ached for any knowledge that might reconnect her with Nathaniel. "And clothes were found in that room as well?"

"I haven't seen the journal, but I assume it's the original and if you go through it, it should contain all that happened. Let's see. An arbor? I don't remember hearing about one in the garden. It must have rotted away if it ever existed...kind of like this house. I think Nathaniel said they married in the garden in the spring."

"April," Rachael murmured.

"Yes, I think he said April. How did you know?"

"It's a beautiful time to be married—just as everything awakens. I'd choose that month myself." Her eyes brimmed.

"As for the diary," Sarah continued, not noticing Rachael's emotion, "I think Nat said he put it in the chest."

Rachael smiled when she heard Nathaniel called Nat by his sister. So unlike her to use diminutives.

"Everything's in the master bedroom closet Nat said. I assume the journal must be there somewhere. Not sure anything in the trunk will help you understand Lady Rachael's life any better, but you are welcome to look through it."

Sarah would never understand how much Rachael knew about Lady Rachael's life. "I would appreciate a chance to do that. I promise I'll be very careful. Will you be here tomorrow? I have things I have to take care of today." She couldn't go through Lady Rachael's personal items today, not after seeing the wedding portrait, it would hurt too much.

"Yes, I'll be here for days." She turned abruptly and was gone.

Rachael was about to leave, but instead moved back in front of the portrait. "Weeks or centuries, real or a dream— I'll never stop wanting you, my love."

Chapter Twenty-Three

The sun sank behind Great Island, swishing its pinks and purples across the clouds and water like a pastel watercolor painting. A nippy May wind blew ripples on the incoming tide. Rachael wrapped her sweater tightly around her as insulation against the chilly breeze. The Cape waters warmed slowly in the spring.

Her afternoon had been spent fending off questions from the local banker about why she wanted to buy such a ruin of a house. She had semi-convinced him that it was worth buying and restoring because the first occupants were such an influence on the town's shipping community and Wellfleet's history. In the end, they agreed on an amount that she could afford to offer for Rose Hill pending an appraisal of the property. She wasn't sure what she would do with the cottage...rent it maybe for a while. She couldn't sell it, too many family memories...when she had a family.

"I visited Rose Hill again today," she said to Kayla as they sat in their usual spots on the deck. She awaited the onslaught of dire warnings. Maybe, just maybe she could ease into talking about her so-called dream.

"Seriously, what in the world do you find so intriguing about that house? I don't get it. You couldn't pay me enough to go anywhere near it. The cobwebs and spiders must be all over the place, ghosts fly everywhere, things go bump in the night...nope, not me," Kay made her usual disgruntled face.

"Someday I'll let you in on the good features of the house, but, in the meantime, I'm doing research on it, the man who built it and the Captain and his lady who lived there."

"Is this going to be based on the old or the revised story? I told you before that I think the grandkids-cubed distorted history to sell that mausoleum. There's something not right about the woman digging in the garden. What's with her? And that grandson-cubed, Nathaniel?" She shivered. "Talk about creepy."

"He's okay. Anyway, about the new story, Sarah said they were cleaning out the house and found a secret room in one of the bedrooms. That's where the wedding portrait, clothes and a new journal were hidden."

"See? Now, number one, who has a secret room in their house, really? And number two, if you do have one, who has the guts to go into it after two hundred years? There could be bodies, giant recluse spiders, ghosts...ugh. Makes my skin crawl." She took a swig of her beer. "And, by the way, was the ink dry on this alleged new journal?"

Rachael couldn't help herself—she had to laugh. Nothing in Rose Hill frightened her. "Your imagination's running away with you. Many older houses had secret rooms for protection in case of an attack. You could use it as a dark room? The house really has a lot of potential. I think with work, it could become that so-called beacon on the hill again."

Kayla snorted. "Really? A beacon on the hill alright, with her ghostly self swinging the lantern? And me working in the hidden chamber? Sorry, not seeing it."

"Well, I can't wait to get in there and investigate every inch of the place. Sarah told me I have carte blanche with the house if it helps me write what I want to write. I agree with you, she's a weird one. I told you I bought the desk in the bedroom?" She sipped her wine. "I hope the Captain's painting comes with it."

"She might be the smart one, wanting to get rid of Ghost Haven. My assessment is that she'd probably make up any story to sell it...it's an albatross for her." She sat for a moment staring at Rachael. "You're the one getting weird—you're obsessed with this Captain guy. What's with that?"

"I'm bewitched." Rachael laughed out loud, thinking how absurd that word sounded in today's world. She sipped her wine again. "Don't you think that sea captains are intriguing? They must have been tough guys to sail through what they had to in those ships." How much did she dare tell Kay? If she let her in on what really happened, would Kayla believe her? This was one time she wasn't sure of Kay's reaction.

"Nothing about Ghost Haven intrigues me, especially dead sea captains."

"I'm seriously thinking of buying the house," Rachael blurted out.

"Oh God, you're kidding, right? I thought you were ragging on me when you talked about making it a B&B. But you're serious? I just don't see it myself."

"I have my reasons and someday I'll tell you, but not tonight." Luckily, her phone rang and cut Kayla off in mid-sentence.

"Rachael?" the deep, sexy male voice asked.

She froze. Her heart hammered…a voice from the grave. "Nathaniel?" she asked, as her wine glass slipped off the arm of her chair with a crash.

"The fourth, remember?" he responded. "Are you okay?" Nathaniel sounded so much like his great-great-great-grandfather.

Rachael laughed as she tried to visualize her Nathaniel trying to use a telephone to contact her. "I'm fine. Just adjusted the phone and dropped my wine glass. How are you? Sarah said you were travelling?"

"I have been."

Rachael waited for more, but he added nothing further about his trip.

"Are you going to be around for a while?" She had no idea what he did for work that caused him to travel so much. If she had to guess, he was following in Nathaniel's footsteps and lived for the sea.

"I'm hoping for no more trips for a while. Sarah said that you wanted to talk? Want to meet at the house tomorrow?"

"I'll be there. By the way, Sarah gave me permission to go through Lady Rachael's things. The ones that you found in a secret room?"

"Lady Rachael?"

She ignored his question. "What time tomorrow?"

"Around two?"

"See you then." Rachael hung up.

"Well, what was all that about?" Kayla asked.

"Nathaniel said that he and I could discuss Rose Hill tomorrow."

"I can't believe the two of you are bizarre enough to want that house." Kayla gulped a mouthful of beer, shaking her head. "I don't think I would ever close my eyes in that place."

"No sleepovers if I buy it?"

"When will you tell me what's behind all this?" Kayla looked serious.

"Soon," Rachael answered. "Very soon. But now I have to sweep up all this glass."

Chapter Twenty-Four

Sarah, dressed in the same dirty jeans, holey gardening gloves and mud-caked boots that Rachael had seen her in time and time again, was sitting on the front stairs of Rose Hill when she arrived at noon.

Rachael plunked herself down beside her. "Hi, Sarah."

Sarah nodded.

"I thought I would begin logging Lady Rachael's belongings before Nathaniel arrives," Rachael began, "if that's okay with you?"

Sarah stood. "Do what you want. I didn't know that Nat was back, but I'll call you when he arrives and the three of us can sit down and discuss the sale of the house. I'm still not sure what he's thinking. I had hoped that this trip would give him time to see how foolish he was being about this relic." She picked up her trowel, waved her dirty gloves and left Rachael sitting on the front stairs.

So much for small talk, Rachael thought.

Sarah shouted over her shoulder, "By the way, if you haven't been out in the gardens yet, you should walk the land if you are thinking of buying this place. It's a beautiful piece of property. Also, you can get a feel for where they were married." She eerily disappeared around the corner and into the bushes.

Sarah had a good point, Rachael had seen the beauty of the land centuries ago, but could it be restored to what it had been? She was nowhere to be seen as Rachael strolled down the weed covered path. She pictured herself walking toward Nathaniel as he waited at the end. He, so handsome in his velvet wedding suit, beamed as she moved towards him. She, so beautiful in the cream silk and Irish lace trimmed gown with her lace train skimming the stone path behind her. It was a dream come true for both of them. Rachael stopped as the footpath became to an abrupt end in a tangle of high weeds. Why couldn't it have been her that day? Why had he belonged to another Rachael?

With the return of the gazing ball, the sun dial, and with hours and hours of weeding and planting, the gardens might resemble what they looked like two hundred years ago. Garden stores must carry heritage plants like the flowers and bushes that were here centuries ago. Sarah might help her as well...maybe?

Rachael spotted what looked like a black wrought iron fence that matched the dilapidated one out front covered in a tangle of vines and brambles. A boundary marker? She made her way through the weeds until she reached a gate. The heavily rusted iron latch wouldn't budge but with a little coaxing, it finally gave way and fell to the ground. Rachael spotted another iron fence further back. It looked like a squared off area... could it be a family cemetery? Her heart hurt as she thought that this might be where Lady Rachael lay forgotten. She pushed through the weeds and brambles until she reached a stone lying on the ground in front of her. She pushed away the vines catching her hands on the thorns.

"Damn it." She sucked on her bleeding finger. "Please don't be Rachael," she prayed as she dropped to her knees. Slowly, letters well worn by time and weather emerged. Mazie.

"Oh no," she cried. "Dear sweet Mazie." And if Mazie was here, Carolyn must be nearby. Scrambling through the brambles on her knees, she found another headstone a few feet away. Pushing the overgrowth away, there stood Carolyn's gravestone.

She dropped back on her haunches, tears filling her eyes. "No, it can't be... you were so young and alive...." Everything was gone, destroyed, dead, even her dream.

"Rachael?"

She froze, afraid to turn. The voice, the time of year, and the place were all too familiar. She touched her denim jeans—no cotton skirt. She turned into the sun, shading her eyes. There he stood, tall and broad shouldered at the bottom of the veranda stairs. The shadows hid his face.

"Rachael, is that you? Are you alright? Did you fall?"

She closed her eyes. The loving way that he spoke her name touched her heart. Another dream? "Please make it be another dream," she begged. "Please let me go back to him." Could it be him? "Nathaniel?" Did he carry a bouquet in his hands?

He strode toward her. "Can I help, Rachael? Did you lose something?" He approached, took her hand and helped her to her feet. "Are you okay? Why are you crying?"

Had she lost something? Was he kidding? She had lost everything. Flustered by how foolish she must look, Rachael sputtered, "It's the sun, it makes my eyes tear." She swiped her cheeks. "An allergy to sunshine. I'm fine. Ah…Sarah told me there had been an arbor out here. I was hoping that I could find where it stood." She couldn't tell him that she cried for Mazie and Carolyn. For some unknown reason, he unnerved her.

"An arbor?"

"Wasn't that where Lady Rachael and Nathaniel were married?"

"Two hundred years ago. But if that structure ever existed, I'm sure it's long gone. This looks like an old cemetery."

"It is. There are a few markers here. Maybe the servants? Or could your great-great-great grandmother be buried here?" She had to know if Rachael laid somewhere in here.

"No, she's not here. Must be the servants. Do you want me to look?"

"No, it's fine. I can do it some other time. Sarah suggested I walk the land if I was thinking of buying Rose Hill, so that's what I was doing when I found this old place."

He held out the flowers to her, violets. "These are for you by the way."

She scanned his face. "My favorite."

"I know."

Was she blurring reality with a dream? "How?"

"Maybe when you talked about Rachael's hand mirror?" He glanced away. "Anyway," he said, turning back, "I know I'm early. I thought you would like to look through Rachael's things while I take care of some estate business. We can talk later?"

"That's perfect. I'd like to take my time, maybe catalogue what I find. Thank you. I'll be in her bedroom if you need me." Rachael breathed a sigh of relief knowing that Nathaniel would be occupied for a while. Reentering the bedroom for the first time would be emotional for her and no one needed to see that, especially Nathaniel. He had already asked enough questions.

As Rachael in the twenty-first century, she had to come to grips with the fact that her Nathaniel, Lady Rachael, and all those that she had come to love, died over two centuries ago. She closed the gate behind her, leaving Carolyn and Mazie to sleep undisturbed.

Chapter Twenty-Five

Rachael arrived on the second floor only to face a closed bedroom door. Someone had rehung it. She knocked, pressed her ear to the door, but heard nothing.

"Hello"' she pressed down on the latch, pushed her shoulder against the swollen wood and flew into a room filled with memories. Nathaniel's voice called her name, pleaded with her to stay. She covered her ears, blocking out his words only to realize that they were inside her head.

Had she done the correct thing leaving him injured? If she had made love to him that night, she wouldn't be standing here today. Would that have been fair to Lady Rachael? But then, she hadn't been very fair-minded with her, placing her in the arms of man like Nathaniel, and then plucking her out of his world and sending her back to an empty life where her heart ached for him every minute of every day. He had loved her and she had adored him.

She sat on the bed where he had struggled to stand, trying to stop her from leaving. The vivid memories made her laugh through her tears. Two hundred years ago she had fallen in love with sea captain. Wouldn't that make a wonderful opening line for her story?

The room appeared shabbier, but unchanged. If the house sold or if Nathaniel decided not to sell, then Rachael would remove the desk, the vanity and the hand mirror to her cottage. If she bought Rose Hill, the items would remain exactly where they were.

Would she be destined to languish as Lady Rachael had if she lived in Rose Hill? Was that the purpose of all this, to return Lady Rachael's life back to her in exchange for her own?

Rachael found herself in front of the vanity. She lifted the mirror. Her tear-filled green eyes and red hair reflected off the tarnished broken pieces of glass. She held her breath, but lightning didn't strike twice.

"There's no returning, is that what you're telling me? I have only memories like you did? Am I destined to be the eccentric cloistered writer in Rose Hill?" She went to the closet. "I won't. I'll find a way back to him—you watch me."

Rachael yanked the swollen closet door open only to face a dark empty cavern. Cobwebs crisscrossed precisely as Kayla had described them. All the dresses, crisp, clean and waiting to be worn, had disappeared. Rachael fell to her knees and wept. How much clearer could it be? Everything was gone and he was dead.

As she peered into the blackness, she knew that she had to do this. Sticky strings stuck to her fingers and something crawled on her hand as she reached into the darkness. She flipped the creature to the floor and wiped the webs on her jeans. She could imagine Kayla's screams filling the house right about now.

Her heart pounded as she reached deeper into the closet. She hit something. It was square, like a trunk. She grappled with the object as she coaxed it along the floor out into the light and into the middle of the room. Carved out of what looked like oak, the sea captain's chest was trimmed with brass and leather. Was it Nathaniel's?

Rachael's smooth hands caressed the scarred worn wood. The tears continued. Enough. Even though her loss haunted her, she had to know what their life was like after she left. The diary must be inside the trunk.

"Rachael, I need to live vicariously through your words."

She tugged on the rusted latch and forced the heavy wooden lid back. It swung backwards, taking her with it. She lost her footing and landed on her fanny with a bang.

"Ouch," she groaned as she picked herself up from the floor, rubbed her backside, and brushed the dust off her jeans. She shook her head; she was still Kayla's klutz.

Inside the trunk, under the first layer of tissue paper, lay a folded, tattered disintegrating white and black muslin dress with hand painted flowers, the same dress that she had worn the night that Nathaniel was shot. There, on the skirt and bodice, was the brown, dried patch of Nathaniel's blood that had stained the dress as she had cradled him on her lap.

It hadn't been a fantasy—she had lived it. Everything she remembered had actually happened in this house. She clutched the dress remnants to her face.

"Oh my God, you did exist." Deep sobs came as she struggled to inhale a slight hint of spice that lingered on the fragments. She remembered how frightened she had been thinking that he would die a second time because of her.

"I wanted you to live, for me... for her," she whispered, resting the dress fragments on the floor.

As she removed more tissue, there laid the remains of the light purple summer dress, one of Rachael's favorites; it made her eyes appear a beautiful violet color. The cloth, faded and torn, almost fell apart as she laid it on the floor. She lovingly arranged the other dresses in the trunk on the floor next to the purple one.

Then she saw it—the wedding gown under a disintegrated pair of silk slippers.

"Oh, how I hated you," she laughed and cried at the same time while gently touching the softly decaying silk. "I couldn't wait to toss you aside." Her tears wouldn't stop at this point.

As she lifted the dress out of the trunk, she heard a thud at her feet—it was a journal. Lady Rachael had tucked it inside the folded gown knowing someday she would find it. Or did Nathaniel?

She remembered standing here on the little stool for hours as Esther stuck her with so many pins during the fitting. Esther was quite the seamstress. Nathaniel had no empathy. He had joked about fitting the material to her body and then kissing away her pain. He had been shameful and she had loved it.

Carrying the dress over to the oval mirror, Rachael held it in front of her. How tiny it appeared. But it was still as breathtakingly beautiful as it had been centuries ago. What a wonderful job Esther had done with all the hand sewing. She had added seed pearls on the bodice and the train that made it even more gorgeous. Lady Rachael must have looked unbelievable in this dress. Why wasn't it she that Nathaniel waited for on that clear cool April morning?

"It would look beautiful on you, Rachael." The unexpected voice froze her. It was her Nathaniel.

"Rachael?"

"Nathaniel?" As she turned, the floor came up to meet her.

The last thing she remembered was the smell of spice enveloping her and the strong arms catching her as she drifted off.

Chapter Twenty-Six

"Are you alright?" Sarah asked, holding a glass of water to Rachael's lips. "Drink," she ordered.

"I'm so sorry. I felt dizzy." Embarrassed, Rachael sat up on the bed, taking a mouthful of water. What a scene she had created. She heard his voice everywhere.

"Maybe I should call the doctor?" Sarah asked.

"No, I'm fine really. I haven't been sleeping well lately and skipped breakfast." She brushed back her hair with shaky hands. "I bent over the trunk, stood up in front of the mirror, and turned quickly. I was lightheaded for a moment," she rambled on.

"You frightened us."

"I feel so foolish." *Us, Sarah said us.*

"I'm glad you're feeling better."

His voice, the tone and the inflections were so real. She hadn't imagined him. She touched her jeans to assure herself that she was still in the twenty-first century. He stood over her—grey eyes flashing with gold, the long nose, the intoxicating smile—it was Sarah's brother, Nathaniel.

"You worried me when you fell," he said. "I barely made it to you before you hit the floor."

"I'll leave you with Nat since your color is returning. Nat, if you need anything, please call me. I'll be right below the balcony. I leave you in good hands, Rachael. When you two decide you need me for the discussion about the house, call me." Sarah left the room.

"I'm so sorry that I made a scene. I haven't been sleeping well as I said… and"—she looked up into the grey eyes framed by long dark lashes—"I guess seeing all these things… they are still so beautiful." She tried to stand, but wobbled a little.

"I think a few more minutes of recovering your sea legs would be advisable."

She laughed, "My sea legs? You certainly are a descendant of a sea captain."

He flashed his grandfather-cube's mesmerizing smile.

His stare made her look away. It was as though he could read her mind and worse still, her heart.

"Sarah tells me that you have been here a number of times since I've been away. She also threw out that you might be interested in buying Rose Hill?"

"I might. She also said that you didn't want to sell."

He hesitated a few seconds and then asked, "What in the world would you do with this place? It needs so much work and it's too big for one person."

"Lady Rachael lived here by herself—granted she had servants and maids to help her. I talked to Kayla about making it into a B&B for history buffs. She wasn't exactly keen on that idea."

His laugh filled her head. "I can only imagine her response."

"But you want to keep it, correct, and live here—alone?"

"If you're asking if I'm single—yes, I am, and would live here alone—possibly." He threw her a mischievous smile and continued, "I have a good reason for wanting to keep this house—my ancestors built it. But explain to me why you're so interested in Rose Hill and my family?"

"As I said, I'm a writer. This is an intriguing historical mystery mixed with romance. Your family combines them both so well. I—I—" she stammered, trying not to show her emotions as she spoke of Rachael and Nathaniel. "The portrait of Rachael alone downstairs intrigued me when I arrived for the estate sale." When she thought of that day, it seemed centuries ago to her. The woman's eyes in the portrait had followed her everywhere. "Then, when I heard Nathaniel had been shot and killed in the house, leaving her unmarried and pregnant, the story really captured me. Rachael had proven herself to be strong in spite of the hardships that she had to endure as a single woman raising her child, their child, alone. It was a story that would ring true for many women today. At least I thought so until…. a new wedding portrait was supposedly uncovered in a hidden room. That wrinkle makes their story so much more intriguing. I would still like to write their story from a more historical view and most of the information resides here, in this house and with you and Sarah. Now that he wasn't killed here, the story changes." She hoped that he believed her excuse. "How could I not be excited to write about all that? Who saved him and how?"

"Supposedly uncovered? You think I lied for some reason?"

"No, I didn't mean that, but it seems strange that your entire family history changed on a dime." She stared at him and continued. "And why had no one ever found this hidden room before?"

"Some things are hard to explain. And I never knew of any hidden rooms when I visited here as a child. There actually might be more, and who knows what they might contain."

"Then I'd suggest that you do more investigation before you sell."

"I guess I might have to. And you've published other stories?" He seemed surprised. "What do you write about—other than lost loves?" His left eyebrow lifted in askance as his great-great-great-grandfather would have done.

She almost blurted out how much he reminded her of Nathaniel but caught herself. "I investigate real people and if their narrative hits me as special, then I write hoping readers will feel the same emotions I did. I do write fiction as well and, yes, I'm published—many non-fiction pieces and a few novels."

"Really? I'm very impressed. I've never met a real author," he paused. "And this so-called love tale of Rachael and Nathaniel that you wish to write about—is it fiction or non-fiction?"

He teased her as Nathaniel would do. "My story would encompass the family's entire history and I never said it was a love story." She tried to trap him. "Wouldn't it be better if it were based on fact? Do you think it's a love story or do you believe like others that he just used her to obtain her father's shipping business?"

"I hope that he loved her and that it wasn't all about ships. I think she continued to run her father's shipping business even after they married as well as running Nathaniel's fleet while he was at sea."

"See, now that would make an interesting story."

"And the non-fiction part of the story, how do you find that since you can't go back to their century? Is it to be told by me, Sarah, and you?"

"Even though Sarah's a duplicate of your great-great-great grandmother—she has her blue eyes, curly hair, and she's tiny—she doesn't speak of either of them and led me to believe that she doesn't think they were a loving couple. And she still seems angry with Nathaniel even though the story has changed and Nathaniel married her." His ancestor's first name slipped off her tongue so easily.

He studied her.

Rachael didn't care what he thought—his great-great-great-grandfather had been hers for a time and she knew for sure that he had loved Rachael with his whole heart.

"Sarah imagines, even with all the new findings, that Nathaniel abandoned Rachael soon after they married, that he left her at Rose Hill to die of a broken heart while he chose to sail the seven seas. She's not interested in the truth"—he hesitated—"as you and I know it." His smoky eyes locked with hers.

"I agree. She doesn't believe that he loved her." She ignored his pointed comment. "Yet, has she even bothered to read Lady Rachael's own words? She could easily read their story as Rachael wrote it."

"As I said, Sarah doesn't care about the truth. To her, for some unknown reason, he was a bastard, probably married Rachael for her father's fortune and once they were married and she was pregnant, he left for parts unknown." He ran his hand along the clef in his chin, his words tinged with anger.

"Was Sarah hurt by a man at some point? It sounds like her feelings about Nathaniel somehow relate to her own life."

"I never thought about it like that. But I have to admit, I know very little about her life. She could have been hurt at some point, but she doesn't share anything personal with me. Maybe she would open up to you if you asked. So, what's your take on all this—the love between Rachael and Nathaniel?"

Was he fishing? Did he suspect that she knew something? "I doubt Sarah will share why she hates him. I believe the truth lies in the journal, in Rachael's own words. Have you read it?"

"I haven't. I don't need to. I believe I know what he was like. But I want to know what you think? Do you feel he was a bastard, that he didn't love her? That he only wanted her fortune?"

"Given what I know about this house, the history, photographs, and the paintings, I believe that he cherished her. What kind of a man searches the lands for Irish lace and Indian silk for his bride's wedding gown?" She smiled remembering the box. "Only a man who loves his lady more deeply than most men today ever could."

He stood waiting for her to finish.

"I believe she filled his mind always as he invaded her nightly dreams." She felt her eyes start to fill as she thought back to the tender man that she had loved, fingering the lace wedding dress lying next to her on the bed.

"Stated like a writer." He offered his hand as she stood. "How do you know about the lace and silk?"

"Can you tell me when they were married?" She sidestepped his question and his extended hand, afraid that if he touched her, she would somehow feel the man that she loved two hundred years ago.

"Rachael's journal should give you the information you want." Nathaniel called his ancestor by her given name as he handed her the worn diary from the floor. "Why do you evade my questions?"

Rachael stood fingering the soft silk of the wedding gown last touched by Nathaniel. "We'll talk after I've read the journal? May I take it home and read it tonight?"

"You may. We can meet back here tomorrow? Maybe you'll answer my questions then? Sweet dreams, Rachael." He turned and left the room.

Chapter Twenty-Seven

The only sound in the house was the rhythmic tapping of Rachael's pencil on the desk as she studied the journal. Using pencil and paper for early notes was an old college habit of hers. Later, she'd sort through them as she filled in her story outline on the computer.

So far, a good picture of Lady Rachael's younger years had emerged, but nothing much about Nathaniel. Hopefully she could find other sources like journals or ship's logs. Nathaniel the Fourth would know of any additional resources that she could use; she would ask when she saw him tomorrow.

As far as Lady Rachael was concerned, she had acquired the expected skills of a well-to-do woman of her era—needlework, music, and the running of a household. But surprisingly, her father had her tutored in mathematics, accounting and history, preparing her to take over his business. Yet, despite all of her education, Nathaniel thought her a spoiled flighty young woman. Perhaps she shrewdly hid how well educated and bright she was from everyone, including Nathaniel. Maybe women who expected to attract a husband couldn't appear brainy. Even today that was true. She thought of Kayla, attractive and very well educated, who had dated a number of men, but scared they away with her knowledge and her outspoken way. Rachael smiled. She had been brainy and Vince had still fallen for her.

"You know who would have been a good match for Kay? Nathaniel's first mate, Dennis. He was as tough as nails, but had a heart of gold... exactly like Kayla," she said aloud, tapping. "Too bad you both hadn't met in the nineteenth century. But then Dennis would be dead and Kayla would be alone too."

Rachael sighed and flipped to the next page of the diary. "But she would have had a man love her, really love her."

It was getting dark so she switched on the desk lamp. She had been at this for hours and knew that the day when she had reluctantly left Nathaniel was fast approaching in the journal. Had Nathaniel made love to Lady Rachael after she was gone? In a bizarre way, she hoped that he had. She had been very brave, saved his life, and deserved a reward. Rachael smiled, wishing it could have been her reaping that compensation. Oh well, maybe she didn't want to read what she had missed. Although it would be interesting to see how Lady Rachael described how she saved Nathaniel.

The front door flew open and a strong wind blew through the house, flipping the pages of the diary.

"Kay, is that you? You could knock, you know?" Rachael waited… no answer. When she looked down, words began to appear, letter by letter as though Lady Rachael stood by her side writing them.

My dear Rachael, I can only thank you this way. You saved Nathaniel and for that I will be ever grateful. You did what I couldn't. And yes, I provided you with my Father's gun to answer your question. I was not strong enough to use it myself, but I knew you could protect him. You are so much tougher than I was. I know you think that you fell in love with Nathaniel, but in time you will find out what really happened. Just know that he and I lived a wonderful life because of you. He was the one and only love of my life and you will find yours soon.

Rachael knotted her hair on the top of her head. Lady Rachael wrote here and now after all these years. How? Rachael picked up her pencil and wrote:

I did what I had to do to protect him. I couldn't let him die again. How could I face having you live all those years alone again without him, being spurned by the community because you had his child? I don't know how you manage to write these messages, but thank you. I will portray your life the way I saw it—you as a strong, caring woman and he as a loving, faithful man. I did love him. I'm sorry.

She waited, thinking what a forgiving woman Lady Rachael was, knowing and seeing how much Rachael had loved her Captain.

Thank you, Rachael. And you did not love him more than I did. Time will soon show you the truth. You have opened your heart again and that's what's important— have a wonderful life, Nathaniel and I know you will.

Rachael stared at the page, stunned once again by the words of this beautiful woman who had died over two hundred years ago. Through her tears, she wrote:

You are very welcome. I have no idea how you do this, but know that your story will be written with love and caring. I will have Nathaniel to help me... your Nathaniel of this century. Thank you, Rachael. I love you both.

Rachael laid the pencil down and waited.

"Rachael? Are you okay?" Kay screamed, running into Rachael's office, her black curly hair standing on end, her backpack sliding down her arms.

"Oh my God, Kay, can't you ever knock? You scared ten years off my life that I can't afford to lose right now," she replied, placing her hand over the writing.

"Knock on what? The front door's wide open. I thought you had been absconded with. Why are you leaving the door wide open?"

Rachael smiled, brushing the tears away. Lady Rachael had entered as usual, blowing through the door. "It must have been one of those ghosts from Rose Hill? Just blew that door open and came in. Maybe the woman with the lantern? Maybe she's still here in the house, Kay."

"Stop. That's not even remotely funny. I swear when I drove by that haunted place last week, I could see shapes and forms and candles fluttering." She flung her bag on the couch. "Please. It's haunted and the descendants— they're even scarier. That loon who digs in the garden and the brother who appears like a ghoul out of the darkness? Weirdoes, that's what I say."

"Did you close the front door, at least?" Rachael asked, laughing. Kayla could be so dramatic. The funny thing was that Kay didn't know that she was correct, even to the candles fluttering that night.

"And I locked it. What are you working so intently on? You didn't even hear me calling you until I stood in this room."

"I borrowed her diary," Rachael said, moving her hand from the journal page. Lady Rachael's words had disappeared.

"Good God, you are obsessed with all this Ghost Haven stuff."

"Maybe I am. But the research on the history of the house and family will be all consuming." Rachael tapped her pencil. "Maybe it will turn out to be at the least a biographical article painting a picture of Rose Hill and the family. And you know as well as I do what an important piece of Wellfleet's history Rose Hill is," Rachael stated, a bit sharper than usual.

"Okay, okay," Kayla put up her hands in surrender as she fell back on the couch, kicked off her sandals and curled up her legs under her. "So, what happened over there today? You buying that museum or just more junk from it?"

Rachael shook her head at Kayla's way with words. "I'm not sure if Nathaniel will sell the property." She sat down next to Kayla.

"Thank heavens. He has less good judgment than you."

"I beg your pardon," Rachael responded, punching Kayla in the arm.

"Ouch," Kayla put on her sad face. "You know what I mean. What would you do in that decrepit old place all by yourself?" She shook her head. "You're pathetic enough now not seeing anyone. Who's going to pick you up for a date at the haunted house?"

"Pathetic, am I? Looks who's talking. And I wouldn't be alone… the lady with the lantern would keep me company at night and the Captain would roam with me during the day…. WoooOOOOooooo…" Rachael joked, but little did Kayla know that's exactly what Rachael hoped would happen if she bought the house. She would return to where she had discovered her true love centuries ago. "Like *The Ghost and Mrs. Muir*, remember that movie?" That was one of her favorite old movies…Daniel, the sea captain, was handsome like her Nathaniel.

"Rachael?"

"Uh? What?"

"Where did you go just now? Stop acting so weird. You're freaking me. And *The Ghost and Mrs. Muir* is fiction, remember? And we agreed that there are no such things as ghosts? So read me some of this inspiring woman's diary. Let's hear this tale of love, death, and resurrection. Geez, maybe I just came up with a name for your story? What'd think?"

Rachael hesitated. Would Kayla make fun of what Lady Rachael had written?

"By the way, I noticed that Vince's Purple Heart box is on your desk?"

Rachael had meant to put it away. Vanessa, Vince's sister, had asked her to attend the presentation ceremony. After it was over, Vanessa handed the blue leather box to her saying, "It really should be with you. He would want that." These last five years it had been tucked away in her night table drawer with her engagement ring, but earlier tonight she had taken it out to the deck, sat and talked to him. She wondered if he could forgive her for falling in love with someone else, even if he was a ghost.

As she held it in her hand and looked into the darkening sky, she saw a contrail illuminated by the setting sun. It resembled a shooting star for just a second. She and Vince loved sitting outside at night searching for shooting stars in the dark heavens. "Make a wish," he would say. "Quick before it disappears. It'll carry your wish forever until it's fulfilled." She knew that he made the same wish every time, that they would be together forever.

"I do love you Vince, but I've been using you as an excuse to hide from life these last few years. That's not fair to either of us. My wish tonight is that you help me to take the next step. I can't do it without your blessing." The contrail faded and blurred in the twilight. Rachael shut the box knowing that she was about to start the next chapter of her life. Her answer came as a shooting star flashed across the darkening sky.

"I've decided to send the medal back to Vanessa tomorrow." She decided that she would keep the ring in her security box; it was all she had left of Vince and he bought it for her. "You were right, Kayla—it's time to move on."

"Hallelujah," Kayla said emphatically. "It sure is about time. I'm really glad that you've finally made that decision. It's been so hard to watch you bubble wrap yourself these last few years."

"I know. But I just couldn't move forward. It was like I needed Vince's approval to do it."

"And?"

"And I think I have it. So that's why the medal's on my desk." She rose, picked up the blue leather box, and carried it to the table by the front door. "I'll mail it off tomorrow."

"I know this is hard, Rachael... but it's the right thing to do."

"I know, but it feels like I'm losing him all over again... this time for good," she said, her voice cracking.

"He'll always have a piece of your heart, but that's okay."

Rachael let out a long sigh. "I have to do it, I agree. So, enough about Vince, let's get back to the journal. I'll read a page out loud, but you have to promise that you'll not say a word, not one single word good or bad. You hear me? I don't want you to ridicule her," she warned and waited, finally adding, "I'm not hearing the promise words."

"Alright, I promise. Jeez, relax." Kayla placed her feet on the coffee table, "Go, I'm all ears."

"Feet down, please," Rachael tapped her feet as she walked to the desk.

"Yes, Mother," Kay mocked Rachael's fastidious nature as she dropped her feet with a bang.

"Remember, you promised?" Rachael ignored Kay's critique of her cleaning habits and brought the diary to the couch.

Kayla nodded.

Scanning the page that had been exposed when the wind blew, Rachael read aloud.

April 20th, how can I ever begin to describe how I feel today, my wedding day, a day I thought I would never see? I feared I would lose my love, Nathaniel, the night that he was shot. I'm not brave, but I have found that I'm smart, smarter than most. I thought that if I couldn't save him, maybe someone else stronger than me could. Working together, Nathaniel and I forced our love to conquer all obstacles—even death. It's impossible for me to find the words to describe how much I love him, how far I would go to protect him, or to keep him alive. There are no words, but I took action.

Today, I walk down the garden path toward the man that I have loved since the day I first met him on the wharf. I was barely sixteen, but even then, I knew I loved him. He and I will join hands, hearts and souls today. Our love will live on forever, through our children and our children's children all because of you.

Rachael grabbed a tissue from the box on the coffee table and cleared her throat. Could she continue without giving away all the emotions that bubbled up inside her right now? She couldn't look at Kayla. Taking a deep breath, she read on:

Nathaniel and I will express our love for all to hear as we face each other today. And when he places his ring on my finger, the circle of our love will join us for all eternity. I wish those who read my words to know that our wedding day is wondrous, truly a miracle on a glorious spring day, sunny and warm, made possible by those who hold the words in this diary to their heart. Know that as I stand in that garden among all the spring flowers, under the blossoms and lace draped arbor and voice my vows, I will never ever forget all that you have done to make this day possible. I take my leave now to marry my Nathaniel.

May my love encircle and protect you even now, as you read this. Thank you....

    Stunned, Rachael looked over at Kayla who waved at her and wiped her tear stained face with the cuff of her sweater.

    The room remained silent.

    Finally Kayla said, "Holy crap. You have to find out what all this mystery stuff is about and who made what possible. You're right—it's a beautiful love story. You have to write it. Oh, to feel that way about a man."

    Rachael touched her opal. "I totally agree.... on all fronts."

Chapter Twenty-Eight

Rachael and Nathaniel sat across from each other at the dining room table where, on a night two centuries ago, Rachael had discussed marriage plans with her sea captain.

"Did you learn anything more about your ancestors when you found those items hidden away in the cubbie?" Rachael asked, clutching the diary against her chest, a pad and pencil on the table in front of her.

"Not much I didn't already know."

"You said you hadn't read her diary?"

He studied her, "No. When I stumbled on that hidden room, I had enough surprises for one day. Did you finish it?" he pointed to the journal that she grasped.

"I was up half the night and still have more to go. Kayla hung around listening as I read and we both ended up crying."

"Because?"

"You have to read her words. She writes so beautifully about their love and life together. You know, you never answered my question yesterday. What do you think of them?"

"Me? I'm positive that he cherished her more than anything else in his world. The sea was his life, but she—she was his love."

He repeated the same words that she had spoken here, in this very room, when she first came to Rose Hill for the estate sale.

He continued on, "When they met, he and her father thought her too young for him, but he couldn't stop thinking about her. He took to the sea hoping that she would mature and not marry before he returned. Rachael, being a good daughter and having great love for her father, cared for him until he died. When Nathaniel received Rachael's message about her father's death, he was halfway around the world. He drove his crew and ship far beyond their capacity, risking all of their lives just so he could return to her. When he finally made port, he found that she was still single and even more bewitching."

He uttered the same words that her Nathaniel had used.

"Bewitching? An interesting choice of words." How did he know all the details? "I thought you hadn't read her journal?"

"I don't need to. My only concern is the truth—that what she wrote in that journal you're holding is the truth."

"Well, I'll tell you what she wrote—she waited for him because she loved him. He was her first and only love. She, in her youth, believed that they could overcome anything as long as they were together."

Nathaniel's face took on sadness.

Rachael waited and then asked, "You lost someone you loved? Were you married?"

"What? No...."

"You looked so sad when I talked about them. Sorry, I didn't mean to pry."

"No. I guess I don't hide my feelings very well. I'll have to be careful around you, you read me too well." His smile never reached his eyes. "Not married."

"But there was a woman?" When he didn't answer, she continued, "I know how that feels. I've lost two good men. I'm sorry."

"You want to talk about them?"

She shook her head. "Not really. I made a stop at the post office before I came here this morning. That completed the story on one."

"Anything I can do?"

"Not unless you can bring them back to life. I'm sorry... I didn't mean to say that. It's been a long time and it's hard to start living again. It was emotional to do what I did this morning, that's all. I'm sorry."

"I understand. Was he the love of your life?"

"My first." She had never had the time to figure out if he was her great love story. "I accepted his ring; he went to war, was injured…and died." She looked at him, wondering why she was telling him all this. "I had to find a way to let go of the guilt."

"Why did you feel guilty? Because you didn't know for sure? He loved you Rachael, and that's all that counts."

"Thank you. Maybe I needed to hear that. I had to close that chapter before I could move on."

"You said there were two?"

"He's gone as well." She laid the journal down on the table. "I'm sorry, I guess my trip to the post office this morning left me with all these exposed threads in my life. Anyway, feeling sorry for ourselves isn't getting your ancestors' story written, is it?"

He nodded.

"Hard not to wonder how things might have been when Rachael's passion seeps through every word she wrote. She adored him; he worshipped her. He would die for her; she would fight to keep him alive. Could there be a more perfectly matched pair?"

Nathaniel stared at Rachael as she added, "How often does a love like that come along?"

"As we both have found out, maybe once every couple of hundred years?"

The flash of gold in his eyes made her heart skip. "Maybe."

The dining room door flew open with a bang causing Rachael to jump up and Nathaniel to leap up and block her from the intruder.

"Sarah, could you give some warning when you are about to fly in? God bless you, you scared the life out of Rachael—and me."

"I didn't realize you were in here. The wind kinda took the door out of my hand. But since we're together, can we talk about getting rid of this place?"

Nathaniel turned to Rachael. "That's my sister. No small talk, just attack."

Rachael smiled and nodded.

"Begin, Sarah. And don't bother apologizing for interrupting our conversation." Nathaniel's words dripped with irritation as he sat back down next to Rachael.

"I said I didn't know anyone was here."

"What do you want to do?" he added disgustedly.

"You know how I feel Nat, I want to sell this place," Sarah stated, sitting down across from them. "It needs too much work and piles of money to make it livable. And since neither of us wants to live here, isn't it foolish to think about keeping it and spending all that money? Our lives are hundreds of miles away. I vote to sell."

"Rachael, your views please?" Nathaniel asked, folding his hands on the table.

A strange dynamic was in play between Nathaniel and Sarah. Rachael had seen them together only once before, when she almost fainted upstairs. Sarah had left the room immediately when Nathaniel spoke up.

Rachael rose and began walking as she always did when she was thinking. "I agree with Sarah that the house needs a lot of work and money to restore it." She held up her hand as Sarah started to speak. "But," she continued, "It does have wonderful bones, irreplaceable historical value to your family and this town. I've spent hours studying what I could of the house and your ancestors. After considering everything, I believe that Rose Hill should be restored to its previous glory. Wouldn't it be terrible if it fell into the wrong hands and ended up being demolished, like that man wanted to do who made you the offer?" She looked at Sarah. "So, given all that, if you both agree, I'd like to buy Rose Hill, if we can work out the terms."

Sarah applauded and turned to Nathaniel who studied his fingers. He rose and held out the chair for Rachael, then moved to the doors where he stood looking out at the overgrown garden and dilapidated veranda.

"Nathaniel, do you agree?" Sarah asked impatiently. When he didn't answer immediately, she addressed him again. "Nat?"

He turned and began, "Sarah, I didn't know there had been an offer on the house?"

"He only wanted the land. I turned it down."

"You should have let me know. I am half owner of this property," he stated. "I didn't even know you were holding an estate sale." He waved her off as she started to speak. "Anyway, let's get back to this discussion. You are both correct. Rose Hill needs an enormous amount of work to restore it."

Sarah interrupted him with her clapping.

His glare quieted her. "And Rachael"—he placed his hand on her shoulder—"you're correct in that Rose Hill holds my family's history, our family history." He addressed Sarah as he continued. "Both good and bad. It's a family as well as a Wellfleet treasure and as such, should be restored to its previous glory as the beacon on the hill. Therefore, I'm not selling." He leaned down and whispered in Rachael's ear, "I'm sorry."

She patted his hand, telling him that she understood.

"What?" Sarah shrieked. "Well, I'm telling you this Nat!" She pounded the table, "I'm not putting one stinking penny into this place, not one. Do you understand me?" She shoved her seat back making a loud scraping noise along the soft pine floor.

As she started to leave, Nathaniel said, "Sit Sarah, I'm not done."

She glared at him. "Don't try to convince me," she growled.

When she sat down, he addressed her, "I'll have the house assessed and I'll buy you out. How's that?"

Sarah was stunned, unable to speak until finally, she asked, "Why...?"

"You don't want it. I do. It's as simple as that. It only seems fair."

"But why, why now? It sat here for years deteriorating and you never cared about it?"

He smiled and looked down at Rachael, "Things change, Sarah. You would never understand if I told you."

Sarah stood. "Nat, I appreciate you being so considerate. I'll finish up my tasks in the garden, we can settle up and I'll be gone." She closed the French doors behind her, crossed the veranda to the stairs, and walked to the garden.

Rachael turned a questioning look on Nathaniel. "What in the world was that about?"

"Don't ask. I can't explain her, never could, never will. Family means nothing to her and that includes me." He sounded disgusted. "Let's go back to our conversation, now that we have settled the house. You know you can have access to whatever you need."

Rachael looked puzzled.

"I'd like you to write their story as well as the history of Rose Hill. Rachael and Nathaniel deserve to live again through your words and have their love, strength, and devotion recorded. You can somehow sense the depth of their feelings for each other. I wasn't sure anyone else could but me. With your own key, you can come and go as you want. You can stay here after I fix her up if that will help your writing."

"Thank you, that's very generous of you. I'll try to do them justice. You can approve the drafts as I write them. We can work together on this if you'd like?"

"Thanks, but I want you to tell their story. As you finish parts, I'll be happy to read and comment on them."

"I have one question. Did Nathaniel have a log or a journal that you know of?"

"A ship's log … I think so. Is there a reason you want it?"

What could she say? That she yearned for any contact with Nathaniel, even his written words describing his adventures?

"It would add depth to their story if we could include some of his thoughts and even trace where his ship travelled and why. There might be some written personal notes? Anything that might improve the manuscript's background."

"I think I know where it is. I'll be right back." Nathaniel left the room.

While she waited, she studied more of Lady Rachael's words starting with the page that she had bookmarked last night with Kayla. Nathaniel was heading back to sea eleven months after their marriage.

Nathaniel left on the morning tide. With baby Nathaniel in my arms and Mazie by my side, I watched his ship slowly sail away until it vanished over the horizon. I can't describe the pain I felt as he disappeared. Oh, how I miss him. He will be away for possibly two years as he sails first south to pick up wood and then to the East where he will trade for tea, spices and silk.

Tomorrow I will return to running my father's fleet, now my ships. I have been delinquent with my tasks for the last few weeks— first with the birth of the baby and then with Nathaniel readying to leave. I have acquired two new ships and now face the task of seeking out crews.

Baby Nathaniel is a beautiful little boy—how blessed we are to have had him survive the birth and me as well. The mid-wife helped all she could, yet it was a long hard birth. By the time Nathaniel returns, the baby will be walking and talking. I will teach him to say Papa as soon as he starts to make sounds.

Rachael could picture Lady Rachael sitting in the parlor cuddling her baby, a cradle at her feet. She would survive Nathaniel's absence and raise her son well. She was self-sufficient, driven by her work and the love of a tall, dark sea captain. She was similar to Rachael in many ways. Maybe that's why she had been chosen to save Nathaniel. They both would do anything to protect the ones that they loved.

The thump of the logbook startled Rachael. She recognized the book as the one that she had fingered in the parlor.

"You were far away just now."

Rachael nodded. "I was, but you brought me back with that thud. Thank you," she joked. "So, let's see what his book has to say."

"Where do you want to start?"

"Can you find his journey before they married? When he went to India and Ireland?"

Nathaniel fingered the pages somewhere near the center of the logbook. Finally, he started to slide the book toward her. "I think this is it?"

"Could you read it out loud please? It will seem more like him talking."

"Sure." He scanned the page, "I'll start on the day he leaves Wellfleet Harbor?" he questioned.

"Perfect."

Nathaniel began to pace as he read.

I see the town drifting away with each moment that passes. I wonder what will befall us as we make our way across the seas. Will we find what we seek for trade? Will we make it home? Will Rachael still be waiting and unmarried?

"He couldn't stop thinking of her even then," Rachael interrupted.

Nathaniel nodded, flipped a few pages, and continued. "This page is entitled 'Bombay 1803.' He writes:

'My men are taking on the rice, cotton, pepper and silk for our voyage home. We leave on the morning tide. While I spent days securing food and water for the next part of our trip, the crew repaired the damage we suffered in a storm we encountered two months ago.

During that typhoon, I feared we might not see another dawn as I stood watch all through the night, strapped to the wheel. The waves rose like black monsters up over our protecting angel, Victoria, her arms outstretched as she tried to hold back the beasts. The lightning illuminated her as she dove down into the black sea and left the beasts to tear at me. And then, as if the behemoths hadn't battered me enough, they tugged on my ropes, trying to take me with them as they receded. The crackling of the masts and the moaning of the ship mixed with the thunder of the storm. As I faced death, my greatest regret was that I did not have Rachael promised to me. I had proposed marriage in passing, but never pressed her for an answer. Only thoughts of returning to her kept me sane during those dark hours and I knew, should I live, I would return and marry her if she would have me.

When I reached the point where I had no more strength to fight off the demons, miraculously, the storm broke and I saw the glorious colors of dawn in the East. I had lived to see another day. We limped into Bombay two months ago. In those two months, I searched out the perfect stones for Rachael's betrothal ring—a unique blue diamond, the color of her eyes, surrounded by sapphires, the color of the sea. And if she has waited and will accept my proposal, I have purchased a bolt of silk that she might use for her wedding dress.'

"He finished the day with those words and set sail at dawn the next morning." Nathaniel stared at Rachael.

She looked down, fumbling with the diary so he couldn't see her tears building. "He loved her so much, didn't he?"

"He did." Nathaniel responded huskily, "Much like your soldier loved you. You shouldn't feel any guilt—thoughts of you kept him alive."

"Until I couldn't."

"That was not your fault, Rachael; you were his inspiration as Rachael was Nathaniel's."

She nodded. "Thank you. I'm so sorry that I'm so emotional today. Is there more?"

"No apology necessary. I think his next stop was Ireland. It was a short stop to look for textile goods and vegetables that would make the trip across the Atlantic."

He flipped more pages and then began.

"We have reached Ireland without much bad weather. We picked up the textiles that are slated for delivery to Boston and delivered the Indian goods to be traded. I was told that one of the most beautiful products here is their handmade lace and so I secured a piece to adorn Rachael's wedding gown. I hope she will be pleased with it. I find myself alone on board. I have no desire to seek a woman other than my Rachael, so I let my men go ashore while I stayed behind with the ship. The crew has done a good job repairing the damage we sustained on this leg of the journey. As I stood on the wharf today, I found Captain Parker walking toward me. He had just arrived from Boston and had a letter for me from Rachael. She wrote that her father had died. I will gather the crew tonight and we will sail at dawn. She is alone now with a

*greedy brother and many who would marry her for her
father's fortune. I hope to reach home and her in time."*

"How long do you think it took him to return to
Wellfleet? Weeks, months?"

"It must have seemed like years to him." He closed
the book and held it out to Rachael. "You said you would
you like to use it to fill in parts of your story?"

"Absolutely. His writing carries so much feeling
like hers did. Are there other books belonging to him?" she
asked placing the book on the table next to her.

"This is his personal journal. There's also a ship's
log where he charts the trip in detail but it contains no
personal information. You can have both, but I thought the
journal would provide more insight into Nathaniel
himself."

"Thank you. You've been so kind and helpful. How
can I repay you?"

He hesitated a minute and said, "Write a wonderful
story."

She nodded.

"There is one thing you can do. Take a walk with
me?"

"Where?"

"Do you feel up to visiting her grave? It's not very
far away. We can talk as we walk."

Could she stand at the grave of the woman that she
had once been?

After a few seconds, she replied, "I could use some
fresh air." She had no choice. She had to visit her.

Rachael pushed Nathaniel's log alongside Rachael's
diary so that the pages touched, hoping their words would
as well. Silly? Maybe, but with what she had experienced
so far in this house, nothing seemed impossible.

Chapter Twenty-Nine

Rachael shadowed Nathaniel along the dark hallway leading to the kitchen. Her hand ran along the dusty worn wallpaper, hoping to feel a lump. Maybe if she found one, she'd be convinced that her Nathaniel had really lived. Had the bullet passed through his shoulder into the wall the first time as well? And he had bled to death because Lady Rachael had run?

"Are you sure you're up for this?" Nathaniel asked as Rachael slowed, her fingers moving, searching.

"Only feeling my way along till my eyes adjust," she lied, her hand resting on a bump in the wall.

"Do you know where he was shot?" Her hand remained on the lump.

"A spot close to you. Legend has it he was defending Rachael. Although, in the light of the new findings, I think it was the other way around—she shot the three men attacking him." He stared at Rachael.

What reaction did he expect? "A woman does what she has to do to save her man, their life together, and their future I guess."

Just talking about it, she could feel the surge of anger that had coursed through her when she faced the men who had shot Nathaniel. And then, they took her anger to new heights when they had the gall to laugh at her. Rage really took over when she saw Nathaniel slump to the floor in a pool of blood.

"Three? Really? I thought she had shot two—one in the leg and one in the shoulder?"

His eyebrow rose with a questioning look. "Actually, now that I think about it, you're correct. Nathaniel's crewmembers apprehended the third man."

Why was he testing her?

They walked through the kitchen and out the backdoor. The barn leaned a bit these days; one of the rotted peeling doors hung by a rusty broken hinge. A slight wind and the entire building might topple. The backyard, overgrown with bushes, weeds and vines was hardly recognizable.

"Dennis." His name just popped out of her mouth.

"Dennis?"

Rachael tripped over a disguised boulder overrun with creepers. A vine scraped across her face. "Ouch."

"Here, let me go first," he remarked, grabbing for her elbow. "Watch out for the rocks," he added, touching her cheek. "You scratched your face. How does it feel?"

"One of the vines… I'm fine," she whispered, moving his hand away, his touch all too familiar.

He placed her hand in his, and said, "It's steep here, so be careful."

If she closed her eyes, she could hear Nathaniel's warning to her two hundred years ago as they had strolled along this same path to his house. He had held Lady Rachael's tiny soft fingers in his large rough hand. His warmth had managed to melt Rachael's frozen heart. But… Lady Rachael had been cruel allowing her to live in her world with her captain. She must have known what would happen, that she would fall in love with him. Rachael's heart ached every minute of every day.

"Are you sure you want to do this, Rachael? We can go back if it's too much."

"No, no, I want to go." He could never imagine what she felt before as they read from Nathaniel's log book. "Can you tell me anything about their wedding?" She allowed him to lightly caress her hand as they made their way along the path. He was her lifeline back to another time and place.

"Rachael chose to be married in the back yard because her father had died and she felt more comfortable walking alone in the garden. They were married—"

Rachael interrupted him, "April twentieth?"

He slowed, but didn't look at her as his hand tightened around hers. "You seem to know a lot about their lives already. How is that?" His voice became almost a whisper.

"Must have been in the part of the diary I read last night," she offered. It was not a lie. "Tell me more about their life, please?" She needed to hear his version of the couple's life.

As they reached Main Street, Nathaniel pointed across the street to the Tavern Restaurant.

"Nathaniel's house. He built it a few years before they married. They lived there when he was not at sea and when he returned to his ship, Rachael moved back up to Rose Hill where she raised their son. She stayed there until she died."

He stopped in front of the house, his eyes travelling intently over each window as though searching for… what? she wondered.

She had walked past this restaurant more times than she could count never knowing its history until she entered the nineteenth century. Was what she remembered a dream? All she knew was dream or not, her heart ached for him, for his touch, and for his kiss. She touched the opal necklace that hung around her neck— Lady Rachael's, but now hers. It hadn't been a dream; it had been real.

"He loved that house so," Nathaniel said out loud, bringing her back to the present.

"Nathaniel, I really do want to buy Rose Hill. It sounds foolish I know, but if I live there and write, I think my words will come easier. The bank okayed my purchase. Maybe the walls will talk to me as my mother used to say."

"I don't know if I can let it go, Rachael. It's my history, my family's past."

"I understand. But you're never here. Will it just sit empty as it has for centuries?" She gazed at Nathaniel's house knowing that it looked exactly the same, a least on the outside.

"Can we talk more when we go back to the house? Maybe we can work something out where I can fix it up and you can live and write there?"

"Rent it, you mean? I couldn't afford to do that and keep my own house. I'd have to rent my house."

"I don't want you to rent it. I don't need the money. It would be nice to know someone was living there, watching over it and it wasn't empty when I'm away. Although even though the ghost roams, I doubt she is capable of fixing much," he joked. "Maybe you could help me restore Rose Hill? Would you be interested in that? It could use a woman's touch."

She laughed. "It needs a lot more than that, but I'd love to help. Do you think we could bring it back to what it was?" She struggled to keep up with his long strides. "And what will Sarah think?"

"You were there when I told her that I'd buy her out. I own it now."

"Sounds like you're going to be the tougher one to negotiate with."

"I have a feeling we can work things out, just you and me. Let's head up this path." He took her elbow and they followed a long forgotten trail that led up the hill behind town.

They climbed silently, lost in their own thoughts—she wondering if she could face her own grave, he…she had no idea what Nathaniel was thinking, but he seemed far away.

"How old was Rachael when she died?" she asked, breaking the silence as they wound their way up the hillside.

"She lived to be ninety-two. Nathaniel died at fifty-six."

"She lived so long without him," she added, remembering the comment that Nathaniel had made on the porch, that maybe he was too old for her. "Are you afraid that because I'm much older than you that you will live a long time alone after I'm gone?"

"She did, she was a young widow—forty-five. Even though their years together were short, they seemed to be happy ones."

"She lived over half her life missing him," Rachael added, as they reached the top of the hill. "But having all those amazing memories of their years together must have kept her warm in winter, as they say."

Nathaniel undid the latch on a low black wrought iron gate surrounding what appeared to be a large family plot. The gate, old and rusty, squeaked as Nathaniel swung it open, the only sound on the quiet hillside. The writing on the array of old headstones and foot markers had been eroded by centuries of wind and rain. The stones, partially covered with emerging spring grass and moss, were unreadable.

"Which is her grave?" Rachael whispered, not wanting to disturb those who rested here.

"Their spot is higher up the hill with a perfect view of the harbor." Nathaniel pointed to a mounded grave site with a rusty old black door built into the hillside above them. It stood above all the others.

"Their spot?"

"What can I say? He never wanted to leave her side, even in death."

"But how?" she whispered, moving toward the knoll. Her tears blurred the worn, rusted words on the tomb door as she approached it. The view in front of where they laid took her breath away—the entire harbor spread out before them, a view past Great Island out to the Bay, the azure blue sky reflected on ultramarine blue water. A slight spring breeze filled with the smell of salt air blew Rachael's hair back. She closed her eyes and inhaled. It made her feel like the girl who lived here two hundred years ago, lighthearted and happy.

"It's a perfect spot for them, so very perfect."

"Nathaniel owned all this land behind his house. When he died, Rachael buried him at the highest point so he could rest watching the ships he loved come and go. When she died, her son placed her next to him and then he donated this piece of the land to the town for a cemetery."

"And their son is buried here as well?"

"That I don't know…possibly but I'd have to research the town's records to find out. He obviously married and had children… a son with my name. I guess that's another project for us to work on—together."

Rachael turned and touched the name. "Mistress Rachael Johnston Haverford," she said her married name out loud.

"A rather big name for such a tiny woman." Nathaniel's voice echoed in her head.

"I'll live up to it, I promise you." She murmured the words aloud, without realizing it.

"And you did, my love." She heard his answer. She turned and saw Nathaniel watching her.

"Captain Nathaniel Rockford Haverford." She ran her fingers over the tarnished raised copper lettering that spelled out his name. "What happened to him, Nathaniel?" Her voice broke, her eyes stung, and her tears built to overflowing as she tried hard to hold them back.

"If this is too much, we can go …."

"I'm sorry. I'm just a little overwhelmed being here where they actually lie," she fibbed. She never lied and yet every question he asked, she answered with a fib.

"He lies here next to her."

"He wasn't buried at sea?" She couldn't take her eyes or her hand off his name. "Oh, thank you God," she prayed.

"He caught a fever somewhere in the South Atlantic, yet somehow willed himself to live until he could see her once more. Within days of arriving home, he died in her arms."

"Oh no…" Rachael sobbed. She should have known that he would come back to her; he always said that he would find his way back. "I will find you no matter what."

"Rachael?" Nathaniel touched her elbow and gently swung her toward him.

"How's it possible that their love story becomes even more beautiful?" She could barely speak.

"Please, don't cry Rachael. They lived a wonderful life. Never have two people been more devoted to each other than the Captain and his Rachael. He loved her from the moment he first saw her."

Rachael smiled, "On the dock." She remembered the story her captain told her on the swing. "You have his full name?"

"Nathaniel Rockford Haverford, the fourth." His laugh reflected the deep rolling one of his great-great-great-grandfather.

"And what do you do, Nathaniel Rockford Haverford, the fourth?"

"I'm an oceanographer. Well, actually a researcher and I own the research ships." He shrugged. "I guess the ocean runs through our veins."

"And you captain one of these ships somewhere out on the seas I imagine?"

"Not anymore. The only ship I captain now is my boat moored at the wharf." He wiped the tears from her cheeks and cupped her chin in his one hand. "Rachael?" he said her name with such reverence, such love.

Can it be? It was her mind playing tricks again. Could she actually be standing here frozen in time between the nineteenth and twenty-first centuries?

Rachael touched Nathaniel's cheek and he moved sensually against her palm.

"What is this? It can't be," she whispered.

"Why?" He touched the collar of her shirt. "Why can't it be?"

She enclosed his hand in hers and held it. Time stopped.

"Do you still have my opal?" His grey eyes flashed gold.

"Oh my God…. How… how do you know about the opal?"

"You took it with you when you left me, didn't you? Lady Rachael searched for it, thinking she had lost it. He bought her another." He squeezed her hand harder. "I had hoped my Rachael had taken it. It was probably the only thing that would help me identify her. It's you Rachael, my Rachael?"

They stood centuries apart, yet touching.

"This can't be…?"

"There was something about you. Each time we were together, I saw or heard something that reminded me of my Rachael. In the bedroom today, when you fainted after you heard my voice, the tears over the dresses, the needing to know what happened to him. It seemed more than just a natural interest, even for a writer. And then you offered to buy Rose Hill or Ghost Haven as your strange friend called it."

"Kayla, dear sweet Kayla."

He laughed, "Or not. I have to admit, you certainly don't resemble my Rachael." He pushed back her wild hair.

Could this really be him? her mind screamed. He was dead. She stood in front of his grave. She had touched his name engraved on his tomb.

"If this isn't a dream, I don't understand what happened then… or now. Do you?" As in a fog, she pulled the opal from inside her shirt, the same one that she held in her hand when she moved from his world back to hers centuries ago. "Oh please, tell me I'm not dreaming, please." She searched his face as the opal flashed brightly.

She would test him. "I'm never without it. It nestles nicely." She had clutched it when she looked into the mirror hoping to have something to remind her that what she had lost was real—not a dream.

"Oh my God, it's you, Rachael." He held her tight, kissing her. "I've searched and searched for you, but had no idea who I was looking for." He covered her face with kisses. "Why did you leave me that last night?"

"Nathaniel, my captain?" Her mind twisted and turned attempting to figure how this dead man stood in front of her, whole, alive and real. "I had to return, but I wanted to stay with you, to make love to you that night. But I knew if I did, I'd never come back here, never. And where would that leave Lady Rachael? I had to go …."

"I wanted you with me so badly. You tore me apart when you left."

"Nathaniel, I don't understand any of this, do you?" She kissed him with the passion that she had felt long ago.

"I fell in love with him, didn't I?" she pointed to the tomb. "Or was it you? I thought that I had stolen him from her and yet knew that I couldn't have him—not forever. I had only borrowed him for those few stolen days. Lady Rachael won in the end."

"No, she didn't. Well, she won because her Nathaniel lived, but it was me you fell in love with… I hope." He wiped away her tears. "I don't have an explanation. For some reason Rachael and Nathaniel needed us to be there at that time and place. I had to save you and you had to save me—well, she and he—and they couldn't do it themselves. They had tried once and he died. Their love was too great to be extinguished by a single misplaced bullet."

"I can't wrap my mind around any of this. For some reason, they chose you and I to relive that moment in time for them? To fix it? To change history?"

"I can't tell you how they did it; all I know is that when I became Nathaniel, he wrote in the logbook that you were not his Rachael, not my great-great-great grandmother. Thank goodness. How weird that would have been, if I fell in love with my great-great-great-grandmother?" He held her face in his hands, staring down at her. "I'm so glad you were my Rachael."

"I agree—very weird indeed. So they found me to play her? The day of the estate sale, she tried to frighten me with blowing doors and writing words that only I could see, sizing me up to see if I was up for the job. They must have voted yea and off I went to the nineteenth century." She shook her head, still unable to understand how her transformation took place. Maybe she never would know. "She used her violet embossed mirror to trap me, knowing that I loved violets. She realized that I'd pick it up. But how and when did he bring you into his life?"

Nathaniel shrugged. "I sat reading his log one night trying to learn more about him since I carry his name, inherited his home, and still own a small part of his shipping business. I know the sea in today's world, but wanted to understand the trials that he had faced during his days at sea." He smiled. "All of a sudden, words appeared on the page. He told me to go to the door of my office and when I did, I turned, the world tilted and there I stood in the cabin on his ship."

"Crafty, weren't they?" She continued, not waiting for his answer. "So you took the ship through that storm? You were the one strapped to the wheel?"

"Yes." He hesitated. "I thought I was going to die out there. I was brought into his life to do something and I hoped it wasn't to die in that storm. His Rachael kept coming to mind and how much he loved her. I knew I had to live." He laughed in her ear, sending chills through her entire body. "If I didn't, how would I have ever met my Rachael? Are you cold?" He slipped his jacket off and wrapped her in the jacket and pulled her tightly to his chest. "I love you, Rachael. I had to find you. You had bewitched me." His deep throaty laugh drifted on the light spring breeze.

She pulled away. "And you mesmerized me, my captain." She stroked his face, making sure he was real. "You at least knew that I wasn't your great-great-great-grandmother, but I thought you were the original captain, her captain." She clasped his face in her hands. "I wish I could have met her. She cared for us and tried to protect us by giving me warnings. She wrote in her journal that danger was coming the night that Philip and his men attacked us. She said to be vigilant, that they were going to try to kill you." She kissed him. "How could I let that happen?"

"When they shot me and I yelled for you to run, I thought that I had failed them. After all I had been through, was I going to die like he did, never knowing who you were, and never changing history?"

"And when you called out for me to run, I started out the dining room door and stopped. If I ran, you would have died as before and I would have failed Lady Rachael. I had to try, do something different. She provided the gun and I chose to use it."

"And my Lady, you were awesome."

"Yes, I was…and I was angry. After it was all over, just before I left you, she wrote that I would return here and find my own Nathaniel. I didn't believe a word of it. How was all that possible?"

"Somehow they brought us together to keep them living and loving in their world for many years. She chose you because she perceived you as being strong enough to stand up to Edwin, Philip and their men. And she chose well, wouldn't you say? And I was chosen because I could survive the sea and the gunshot wound—with your help. We gave them back their lives, Rachael, and in return, they gave us ours."

Rachael turned and touched the names engraved on the rusting door. "I've missed you so much, Nathaniel. I dreamt of you, heard your voice at night…I fell in love with a man I thought lived and died over two hundred years ago."

"Why did you come back here? I would have easily taken over their lives if I could have had you."

"I almost stayed. We could have lived out their story so easily, but it wouldn't have been right. That would have been their lives, not ours. And that was the decision I made that night… to return Rachael's captain and her life back to her."

"Nathaniel promised I'd find you again. I told him I didn't want to leave you. The old sea dog actually sounded amused that I had fallen in love with you; amused and quite pleased that we had fixed their lives and they had fixed ours." He kissed her lightly on the lips. "I left their world right after you did. I didn't know how I would find you. I knew nothing about you… where you lived, what you looked like…. Only that I had fallen in love with the woman who lived inside my great-great-great-grandmother." He pushed back her hair slowly. "I love the color of your hair, by the way. You are quite my match, I think." He pulled on her curls. "It might take me a bit to adjust to your height, though," he joked.

"Oh really? Well, I have no adjustments at all. You're a clone of my captain."

"I gave up the sea for you. When I came back here, I hoped foolishly that I might bump into you on the street, in the market, or find you on a beach. But, after weeks went by, I began to feel it wouldn't happen, that I'd never see you again. I had no idea who I was looking for. I only knew you as a petite blonde. I, at least, resemble him, a little."

"A lot. Your laugh, your voice, your quirky eyebrow and adorable cleft chin are his." She touched his clean shaven face. "I'm so glad you shaved off your beard centuries ago so I could see your features clearly." She fingered his eyes, his nose, and his lips. "You are different from him in that you gave up the sea to find me."

"He had no choice, you know that, Rachael. That's the way he made his living."

"I know and more importantly, she knew. When I returned home, my life seemed so empty. I stood day after day wishing your white sails to appear on the horizon. I knew better, but stood there anyway. I recreated Rachael's garden in my backyard in hopes of what? Remembering? I didn't need anything to remind me of your voice and touch. Today, as I knelt at Mazie's grave and you called, I had hoped that lightning would strike again…take me back to him, I prayed. I greedily sought Lady Rachael's life, but there was nothing I could do to recapture it. I had saved you for her even though it was me who had loved you." Her eyes welled up.

"Had?"

She smiled. "What made you think I was her?" she whispered.

"In the bedroom, I watched you tenderly touch the clothes, especially the dress that you wore the night I was shot. You held it up to your face and I saw the tears. When you stood in front of the mirror hugging the wedding dress, the sadness in your eyes broke my heart. Then, when I spoke and you turned, I saw a flash of her blue eyes behind the tears. They had chosen us to make their love endure."

The love from long ago spread across his face. "I never saw you in the wedding gown. And poor Esther worked so hard on it. Will I ever see you wear it?"

"Dear sweet Esther, she created a gorgeous dress, didn't she? I wonder if she ever married?" She looked to Nathaniel.

"I hope so, I don't know. More research for you to do? And you avoided my question? Am I going to have to beg once more?" His raised eyebrow signaled a throwback to her Nathaniel.

"For the Rachael of today to fit into that gown, she'd have to shrink six inches and lose twenty-five pounds. But with family approval, we could find a today's Esther and have it remade for someone taller? What do you think?"

He placed his arms around her. "I think that if you tailored it, my great-great-great-grandmother would love it."

"And, did you choose the silk and the lace for her? And the stones for her ring?"

"When I entered Nathaniel's world, he wrote that I had to help him stay alive no matter what and that when I returned to Rose Hill, Rachael, my great-great-great grandmother, would be inhabited by someone else. He itemized the places I had to stop and what had to be done when I arrived. One thing I had to do was design a betrothal ring for his Rachael. He had some rough drawings on his desk—I enhanced them a bit." Reaching into his pocket, he removed a blue velvet box.

"You still have it? Oh my God, I must be dreaming. None of this can be happening. Please tell me I won't wake up without you? Or I'll turn and you'll be gone?"

"No dream, Rachael. And I'm not going anywhere, not leaving your side ever. You better make sure that's what you want. I have her ring," he said there in front of Rachael and Nathaniel's tomb. "Night after night, I stayed awake thinking I would never find you, that I'd never have a chance to place this ring on your finger—this time for us. I fell in love with you, Rachael..." He laughed "I don't even know your last name, do I?"

"Rachael Corbet."

"Rachael Corbet, I fell fiercely in love with you centuries ago, as you masqueraded as my ancestor. You were quite unique—feisty, unafraid, and quite forward. Not sure those were good qualities back then, but I digress."

Rachael pinched his cheek. "Please continue."

He laughed, "You make me bare my heart once again?"

"I do...please ask me... for us."

"You invaded my thoughts every minute of every day; you bewitched me, and intoxicated me." He laughed. "How ridiculous those words sound today, don't they?" He took her hand.

She started to interrupt, but he hushed her. "You have to let me say this."

She nodded.

"I remember the first time I saw you in the garden with Sarah. You spoke so lovingly of Rachael and Nathaniel, with such sadness. Sarah didn't notice, but I did. I stood outside the living room when you saw their wedding portrait for the first time and you realized that we had changed history—somehow. I watched you search through her clothes for something that would bring you back ... to me."

She brushed his hair back off his forehead. "May I speak now?"

"Please, my lovely Rachael. Bewitch me."

"I didn't believe any of it until I saw their portrait. I kept telling myself it was a fantasy...that it couldn't have happened. But that portrait portrayed their love so perfectly...our love story," she laughed. "All of our love stories. After I left you, I mourned you because I believed that you had died long ago, lost at sea, and you laid somewhere on the bottom of the Indian Ocean. I cried because I couldn't visit your grave. Lady Rachael never told me that you weren't her Nathaniel. So when I left, I thought I was leaving her Nathaniel behind. I was sure that night that you knew I wasn't the real Rachael and that I was going away. I thought I had stolen you from her."

"I told you that I would search to the ends of the earth for you."

"I know, but I didn't know what that meant until I had returned home. I thought you remained behind with her."

"When I stared into your eyes in Rachael's bedroom today, I knew it was you." He wiped her tears away, brushing his lips lightly over hers. "I have missed you so much, my beloved Rachael."

She wrapped her arms around his neck. "How lucky I am to love the same man twice, two centuries apart," she whispered in his ear. "She told me I would find you and live happily ever after, but I didn't believe her. They brought us together at Rose Hill." She turned and faced Rachael's and Nathaniel's tomb. "Thank you from the bottom of my heart for keeping your promises."

"But we'll have to make the rest happen ourselves." He turned her to face him and went down on one knee. "My beloved Rachael, will you wear this ring as a token of my undying love? Will you marry me?"

"Please place the ring on my finger?"

He slipped the striking blue diamond solitaire surrounded with shimmering sapphire baguettes on her finger. It sparkled in the sunlight as her Captain had described—the color of her eyes surrounded by the sea.

"I love you, Nathaniel Rockford Haverford the fourth. I will wear this ring until the day I breathe my last." Her tears began again, but this time from happiness.

He rose and kissed her. He moved behind her as they faced the sea together, his arms wrapped around her, his chin resting on her head.

"Please don't leave me—ever."

"How could I when you bewitch me all over again," he whispered in her ear, turning her to face him.

"I couldn't fathom living without you, Nathaniel. I was so lost." His voice brought her back to 1804 and the taste and feel of her Captain. "Somehow they orchestrated their entire past and our present and still-to-be future. I loved you then and love you more now. You make me laugh like you did centuries ago. The messages she wrote that only I could see, they came and then disappeared. I wrote back to her and somehow she could read my words as well. She warned me of Philip and of the danger from your crewmember. I wrote and apologized to her the night that I left you. I told her I had fallen in love with you. She quickly wrote back that wasn't true, that I would find my own happiness. How could I have doubted her, she choreographed everything so perfectly."

Rachael placed a kiss on their names. She cried for this couple that she had grown to love and admire. They knew what they had and fought hard to keep it, even to the point of changing history so they could be together.

Nathaniel took Rachael's hand. "Let's leave Rachael and her Nathaniel to rest in peace now that they have seen to it that we are together." He spoke in hushed tones as if not to awaken them. His face reflected his great-great-great-grandfather's youth and vitality.

They stood arms around each other looking out to the sea, the same sea that they had viewed together so many years ago, and then they started back down the hill.

"Can you imagine Kayla's face when we tell her this story?"

His smile said it all. "Oh, what fun it's going to be. She'll never believe that I'm from this century."

"Should I text her?"

"Sure."

"Let's take a photo." Rachael took out her phone and clicked a photo of them, heads together with the harbor behind them.

Rachael typed, "Am with the Captain now. We are to be married. Will you be my maid of honor?" She placed the phone back in her pocket.

"Aren't you going to wait for an answer?"

"Nope. I know her too well. When she reads it, we'll hear her scream all the way up here."

"Well then, since I now own Rose Hill, shall we live there my love, or would you be more comfortable elsewhere? I could buy my great-great-great-grandfather's house back?"

"Rose Hill…my Captain, Rose Hill."

Eleven Months Later…

The Cape Cod Weekly

Wellfleet – On April 20th, Rachael Ellen Corbet and Nathaniel Rockford Haverford IV were joined in marriage under a rose covered arbor in the spring gardens of Rose Hill. Following the ceremony, a reception for family and friends was held under a tent in the back yard which overlooks Wellfleet Harbor.

Rachael wore Nathaniel's great-great-great grandmother's wedding gown and carried a bouquet of yellow roses and tulips mixed with purple violets. She walked the identical path that Lady Rachael Johnston had walked on April 20th 1804 when she wed Captain Nathaniel Rockford Haverford. The couple exchanged the wedding rings that Nathaniel's ancestors had worn over two hundred years ago.

Kayla Rebecca Simon served as Rachael's Maid of Honor. Dennis Edward Faraught IV, great-great-great grandson of Dennis Faraught who served as Captain Nathaniel Rockford Haverford's first mate, acted as Nathaniel's best man.

Rachael, who owns a home in Wellfleet, is a graduate of Simmons College and Boston College. She is a freelance writer. Her latest book, A Never Ending Love: the story of Rachael Johnston and Nathaniel Rockford Haverford *can be found on the NY Times Best Seller List.*

Nathaniel, whose Wellfleet roots extend back to the 1700s, has degrees in Oceanography from University of CA (BS), University of WA (MS) and UC San Diego, Scripps Institution of Oceanography (PhD). He owns and operates a family shipping business and performs research at the Woods Hole Research Center where he serves on the Board of Directors.

For their honeymoon, the couple will recreate the trading trip that Nathaniel's great-great-great grandfather took to Ireland and India to secure material for his bride's wedding gown and the stones for her betrothal ring.

The couple will reside at Rose Hill where they first met years ago.

About Judi Getch Brodman

Judi's software consulting work has taken her all over the world even out to the Marshall Islands where she flew to work each day. Her bookshelves are filled with photographs and journals that capture her experiences and feed her imagination as she writes. But her roots and true inspiration come from New England, in the mountains of Vermont and by her childhood beaches of Wellfleet on Cape Cod.

In 2011, she began her writing journey with three published travel articles on Ireland, The Many Faces of Ireland, followed by a short story, Safe Harbor, published in July 2012. Then, inspired by the death of her sister in 2015, Judi wrote and published two children's books, "Fiona - the Lighthouse Firefly" and "Fiona the Firefly - LOST!" both titles available on Amazon, the proceeds of which feed a scholarship fund that Judi set up in her sister's name. Scholarships are being awarded to students studying Business and Technology.

In her spare time, Judi is a professional watercolorist, reads, walks, gardens, and enjoys family and friends. But wherever she is, her characters and their magical worlds fill her mind.

Judi has been involved with writers' groups for years, has taken Creative Writing at FAU, and has worked with authors in workshops whenever possible. She's also an editor for Wiley's technical magazine, Journal of Software: Evolution and Process.

Her debut novel (She's Not You - a mystery with a splash of romance), has received excellent reviews from her readers...

"Seriously, I loved the story, it's twists & turns and the ending leaving room for book 2 which I will await anxiously !"

"I was engrossed & couldn't put it down!"

"It built up in mystery and emotion and certainly was tense at the finish."

Social Media

All Author: https://allauthor.com/profile/judigetch/

Blog: https://judigetchbrodman.wordpress.com/

Facebook: https://www.facebook.com/judigetchbrodman/

Solstice Publishing:
http://www.solsticeempire.com/products.aspx?categoryid=194

Acknowledgements

I need to thank my editors and proof readers at Solstice Publishing for taking the time and effort to make this book the best that it could be.

I also need to thank my family for all their support and encouragement. They are always cheering me on.

And I can't forget my writers group and writing coaches through the years… their constructive criticism has made me a better writer.

And last, but certainly not least, my husband Steve who always loves and supports me, and promotes me as "a

Renaissance woman."   I love you very much and thank you for traveling this road with me!

www.ingramcontent.com/pod-product-compliance
Lightning Source LLC
Chambersburg PA
CBHW051138020726
47501CB00005B/1564